THE
LUCKY BAG

'When I was a child you could buy lucky bags
for five pence. They had chewing gum, a brightly
coloured gob-stopper, a wine gum and something smooth and
chocolate. This literary lucky bag has the exotic and the
chewy, the flavoursome and the plain in it. It whets
the appetite and sharpens a sweet tooth.
The Lucky Bag introduces its readers to their very
own cultural history and shows them a world that
sets them apart and makes them special.'
ULSTER TATLER

'a well stocked and surprising bag'
THE SCHOOL LIBRARIAN

D1080861

O'BRIEN PRESS AWARDS

IRISH BOOK AWARDS – 1985
Best Illustrations

THE LUCKY BAG, Classic Irish
Children's Stories
Ed. Eilís Dillon, Pat Donlon, Patricia
Egan, Peter Fallon
Illustrated by Martin Gale

READING ASSOCIATION OF IRELAND
AWARD 1987

CYRIL, The Quest of an
Orphaned Squirrel
by Eugene McCabe

IRISH BOOK AWARDS –1988
Silver Medal

BIKE HUNT
by Hugh Galt

READING ASSOCIATION OF IRELAND
1989 – Special Merit Award

EXPLORING THE
BOOK OF KELLS
by George Otto Simms

BISTO BOOK OF THE DECADE AWARD
1990 (Irish Children's Book Trust)
Joint Winners

EXPLORING THE
BOOK OF KELLS
by George Otto Simms

BRENDAN THE NAVIGATOR
by George Otto Simms

BISTO BOOK OF THE YEAR AWARD
1991 (Irish Children's Book Trust)
(Best emerging children's author category)

BRIAN BORU
Emperor of the Irish
by Morgan Llywelyn

INTERNATIONAL READING
ASSOCIATION AWARD – 1991

and

READING ASSOCIATION OF IRELAND
AWARD – 1991

and

OSTERREICHISCHEN KINDER UND
JUGENDBUCHPREIS – 1993

UNDER THE HAWTHORN TREE,
Children of the Famine
by Marita Conlon-McKenna

BISTO BOOK OF THE YEAR AWARD
1992 (Irish Children's Book Trust)
Best Historical Novel Category

WILDFLOWER GIRL
by Marita Conlon-McKenna

BISTO BOOK OF THE YEAR AWARD
1993 (Irish Children's Book Trust)
Overall Winner

THE BLUE HORSE
by Marita Conlon-McKenna

BISTO BOOK OF THE YEAR AWARD 1993
(Historical Fiction Category)

and

READING ASSOCIATION OF IRELAND
AWARD – 1993

STRONGBOW
by Morgan Llywelyn

THE
LUCKY BAG

THE
LUCKY
BAG

CLASSIC IRISH CHILDREN'S STORIES

Introduced by
EILÍS DILLON

Edited by
PAT DONLON, PATRICIA EGAN

EILÍS DILLON and

PETER FALLON

Illustrated by
MARTIN GALE

THE O'BRIEN PRESS

First published 1984, The O'Brien Press Ltd.,
20 Victoria Road, Dublin 6, Ireland

First paperback edition 1987
Reprinted 1988

© Copyright to this collection, the illustrations,
and translations, held by The O'Brien Press;
copyright to other stories
held by the authors or their representatives
or executors. For a full list
of acknowledgements, see page 200

All rights reserved. No part of
this book may be reproduced or utilised
in any form or by any means, electronic or mechanical,
including photocopying, recording or by any
information storage and retrieval system
without permission in writing
from the publisher.

British Library Cataloguing in Publication Data
The lucky bag: classic Irish children's stories.
—(Lucky tree books, ISSN 0790-3669)
1. Children's stories, Irish
I. Title
823'.01'089282[J] PZ5

ISBN 0-86278-135-3
10 9 8 7 6 5

The O'Brien Press acknowledges the assistance of
The Arts Council/An Chomhairle Ealaíon, and the
Arts Council of Northern Ireland in the publication of this book.

Book Design: Michael O'Brien
Typesetting: Design and Art Facilities
Set in Palatino
Printers: The Guernsey Press Co. Ltd.,
Guernsey, Channel Islands.

Inside The Lucky Bag

The Editors

Eilís Dillon was born in Galway in 1920. She has written many novels including *Across the Bitter Sea, Blood Relations* and, most recently, *Citizen Burke*. Her popular children's stories include *The Lost Island, The Island of Horses* and *The Cat's Opera* which has been adapted to the stage.

Pat Donlon, Ph. D., is Director of the National Library of Ireland and was Curator of the Western Collection at the Chester Beatty Library. She has written and broadcast extensively on children's books, and compiled with Maddy Glas *Moon Cradle*, a book of lullabies.

Patricia Egan, who compiled a bibliography of 19th century Cork authors was Executive Librarian in Cork City Library. She is a frequent reviewer of children's books. She has worked on the first translation into English of *Jimín Mháire Thaidhg*.

Peter Fallon, a poet, was born in 1951. In 1970 he founded The Gallery Press in Dublin and he continues to edit and publish Gallery books. He lives on a farm in Loughcrew in County Meath.

The Illustrator

Martin Gale was born in England in 1948 but has lived in Ireland since 1950. In 1980 his paintings represented Ireland at the Paris Biennale. The following year the Irish Arts Council arranged a touring exhibtion entitiled *Family and Friends*. His paintings are featured on the covers of several titles in the classic Irish Fiction series. A member of Aosdána, he lives in County Wicklow.

Introduction: To the Reader *Eilís Dillon*

WHEN I WAS SMALL, there were two kinds of lucky bag, one
for a penny and one that cost twopence. The smaller one
was diamond-shaped, with a bright, cheerful design on the
cover, and it always contained a tiny toy as well as some
miniature sweets that one never saw anywhere else. The
twopenny one was thicker, longer and more substantial, its
cover was more staid and its contents were naturally more
complicated and its sweets bigger. It might contain a
Japanese paper flower which unfolded when it was dropped
into a glass of water, or a puzzle that took some time to work
out. Once I had one that had to be opened very carefully
because a rabbit made of cotton wool, with long ears and
wearing a dressing-gown, had somehow been stuffed into
it. I never thought the big one was better than the small one:
it was just different.

We have named our collection *The Lucky Bag* because it
contains a variety of surprises. Some you will find quite
complicated, others so simple that you may wonder why we
put them in at all. One thing they all have in common is that
they are Irish, and that means that they are good stories in
the sense that you will never be bored by them. In Ireland
we all love a good story, whether it be about ghosts and
magic and strange, inexplicable happenings, or about the
ordinary doings of everyday life. Some of these stories
combine the two elements very successfully.

The oldest story in the book is a piece from *Gulliver's
Travels*. Jonathan Swift was the Dean of St Patrick's
Cathedral in Dublin from 1713 to 1745, when he died.
Gulliver's Travels was written when he was quite old. It was
intended to show how ridiculous it is for people to put on
airs, and try to make themselves look important by dressing
in fine clothes, wearing crowns and long, trailing robes, or
uniforms covered with medals. Captain Gulliver is cast
away on an island where everyone, including the king, is no
more than six inches tall. Then, on another voyage, he lands
on an island where the people are twenty feet tall and think
he is a miserable little insect. A third voyage takes him to a

land where the horses live in houses and the people in the fields. Swift had endless fun with the possibilities of these situations, and he told his stories so seriously that a great many people of his own time believed them to be true. They were not written for children at all but like most good books they were enjoyed by people of all ages.

The power to grip your audience is the whole secret of story-telling. In the days when stories were told in the evening, around the fire, it was just as important as it is now. The old story-tellers knew how to begin: 'There was a man once, and he was walking home alone one stormy night.' You may be sure that no one would move until they found out what happened to that man, whether or not he got home safely, why he was out so late, why he was alone instead of with a crowd of his friends, how long he had been away from home and a whole list of other questions that were raised at once by the story-teller's first words. Mary Lavin is an expert at this. A great many of her stories, like the one we have included here, 'A Likely Story', are about people who are going along quietly, leading rather ordinary lives, making little plans for the future, surrounded by people they have always known, until one day something happens to show them that things are not quite what they seem to be. In this case it is the widow's son, Packy, who makes the discovery, but he will never be able to convince his mother of it.

Some of the stories are written as if they were being told around the fire in the old way. One of these is Eileen O'Faoláin's 'Cliona, Fairy Queen of Muskerry'. The old woman, Biddy, is telling the story to two children who have dropped into her cottage for a chat. Her pet hen, Cossey Dearg, is on her perch in the kitchen, and seems to be listening too. Since the story concerns her own fate, she does well to take an interest. Biddy uses her everyday way of talking and we soon feel we're in the kitchen with them.

In 'A Stocking Full of Gold' Kathleen Fitzpatrick uses the same method. Lull, the maid, knows far more about the countryside and its people than the children, and they rely on her to tell them the important things that they would never hear otherwise – who is sick, who is dying, who is needing help from the neighbours. That story has a happy

8

ending, but another of the same kind, 'The China Doll', is very sad, even harsh, except that we somehow know that Mary-Ellen who is telling it was able to bear her unpleasant experience, though she never forgot it. There are plenty of stupid, cruel people in the world, and we must all try to live with them – not too close – as best we can. With a story like this one, the depth of the impression is more important than whether or not it has a happy ending.

We are very glad to be able to include Micheál mac Liammóir's story 'St. Brigid's Eve', first of all because it has been out of print for a long time and there was a danger that it would be forgotten, and also because it has an historical value. It was written and illustrated when the author was seventeen years old, in the very early days of Irish independence, when Irish arts and the Irish language were beginning to be valued again. It is one of four stories in a book called *Faery Nights*, each concerning a special night when the fairies are abroad. Micheál mac Liammóir was known internationally as an actor, playwright and producer, and in Ireland as the founder of the Dubiin Gate Theatre.

A good many of our stories were not written specially for children at all but, like *Gulliver's Travels*, can be read by everyone. Seán O'Faoláin's 'The Trout' is one of these. He is one of the great short-story writers of the world and has written an excellent book about story-telling. You will notice that as the story goes on, we find out more and more about Julia, so that we know long before the end what she is likely to do – we know what kind of person she is. We hope she will do something sensible, and she does.

In the same way, but for a different reason, we are on the side of the small boy in Frank O'Connor's 'First Confession'. The priest, the very person that his horrible sister was threatening him with, comes to his aid and gives us double satisfaction. Brian Friel's story, 'The Potato Gatherers', and my own 'Bad Blood' show boys on the edge of being grown up and learning to handle the good and the bad aspects of being a man.

We hope that all of these stories will lead you to search for more work by the same authors. One book, or one story, should always lead to another.

Mary Lavin (1912-   )
Mary Lavin's perfectly simple story of the widow and her son, Packy,
begins like many of the best stories 'Once upon a time...'. It is set in the
shadow of the old Abbey at Bective in County Meath beside
Mary Lavin's farm.
Mary Lavin was born in America but has lived most of her life in Ireland.
Her stories are known all over the world.

A Likely Story
Mary Lavin

ONCE UPON A TIME there was a widow who had one son. He
was her only son: her only joy. His name was Packy. Packy
and the widow lived in a cottage in the shadow of the old
abbey of Bective. The village of Bective was opposite, on the
other side of the river Boyne.

Do you know Bective? Like a bird in the nest, it presses
close to the soft green mound of the river bank, its handful
of houses no more significant by day than the sheep that dot
the far fields. But at night, when all its little lamps are lit,
house by house, it is marked out on the hillside as clearly as
the Great Bear is marked out in the sky. And on a still night
it throws its shape in glitter on the water.

Many a time, when the widow lit her own lamp, Packy
would go to the door, and stand on the threshold looking
across the river at the lights on the other side, and at their
reflection floating on the water, and it made him sigh to
think that not a single spangle of that golden pattern was
cast by their window panes. Too many thistles, and too
many nettles, and too much rank untrodden grasses rose up
in front of their cottage for its light ever to reach the water.

But the widow gave his sighs no hearing.

'It's bad enough to have one eyesore,' she said, 'without
you wanting it doubled in the river!'

She was sorely ashamed of the cottage. When she was a
bride, its walls were as white as the plumage of the swans

10

that sailed below it on the Boyne, and its thatch struck a golden note in the green scene. But now its walls were a sorry colour; its thatch so rotten it had to be covered with sheets of iron, soon rusty as the docks that seeded up to the doorstep.

'If your father was alive he wouldn't have let the place get into this state,' she told Packy every other day of his life. And this too made him sigh. It was a sad thing for a woman when there was no man about a house to keep it from falling down.

So, when the rain dinned on the tin roof, and the wind came through the broken panes, and when the smoke lost its foothold in the chimney and fell down again into the kitchen, like a sack of potatoes, he used to wish that he was a man. One day he threw his arms around his mother's middle.

'Don't you wish I was a man, Mother,' he cried, 'so I could fix up the cottage for you?'

But the widow gave him a curious look.

'I think I'd liefer have you the way you are, son,' she said. She was so proud of him, every minute of the day, she couldn't imagine him being any better the next minute. He was a fine stump of a lad. He was as strong as a bush, and his eyes were as bright as the track of a snail. As for his cheeks, they were ruddy as the haws. And his hair had the same gloss as the gloss on the wing of a blackbird.

'Yes, I'd liefer have you the way you are, son,' she said again, but she was pleased with him. She looked around at the smoky walls, and the broken panes stopped with old newspapers. 'What would you do to it, I wonder – if you *were* a man?'

Her question put Packy at a bit of a loss. Time and again he'd heard her say that all the money in the world wouldn't put the place to rights.

'Perhaps I'd build a new cottage!' he said cockily.

'What's that?' cried the widow. But she'd heard him all right, and she clapped her hands like a girl, and a glow came nto her cheeks that you'd only expect to see in the cheeks f a girl. 'I believe you would!' she cried, and she ran to the loor and looked out. 'Where would you build it, son? Up ere on the hill, or down in the village? Would you have it

11

thatched, or would you have it slated?'

'Slated, of course,' said Packy decisively, 'unless you'd prefer tiles?'

The widow looked at him in astonishment. Only the Council cottages had tiles.

'Would there be much of a differ in the price?' she asked timidly.

'Tiles would cost a bit more I think,' Packy hazarded. 'And they mightn't be worth the differ.'

A shadow fell on the widow's joy.

'Ah well,' she said. 'No matter! If we couldn't do everything well I'd just as soon not build at all! I wouldn't want to give it to say that it was a shoddy job.'

There would be nothing shoddy about it though.

'I was only thinking,' said Packy, 'that it might be better to put the money into comfort than into show. We might get a range in the kitchen for what we'd save on the tiles!'

'A range?' cried the widow. Never, never, would she have presumed to think that she, who had stooped over a hob for forty years, would ever have a big black range to stand in front of and poke with a poker. But all the same she felt that it might be as well not to let Packy see she was surprised. Better to let him think she took a range for granted. So instead of showing surprise she looked at him slyly out of the corner of her eye. 'What about a pump?' she said. 'A pump in the yard?' But she saw at once by the way his face fell that she'd gone a bit too far. The Council houses hadn't as much as a mention of a pump.

'I thought maybe it would be good enough if we built near the pump in the village,' Packy said uneasily.

'Sure of course it would be good enough, son,' she conceded quickly. After all, a pump in the yard was only a dream within a dream. But she would have given a lot to stand at the window and see her neighbours passing on their way to the pump in the village, and better still to see them passing back again, their arms dragging out of them with the weight of the bucket, while all she'd have to do would be to walk out into her own yard for a little tinful any time she wanted. It would make up for all the hardship she'd ever suffered. Oh, she'd give a lot to have a pump in her own yard!

12

And looking at her face, Packy would have given a lot to gratify her with a pump.

'I wonder would it cost a lot of money?' he asked.

'Ah, I'm afraid it would, son,' said the widow, dolefully. Then all at once she clapped her hands. 'What about the money we'll get for this place when the new cottage is built? Couldn't we use that money to put down a pump?'

Packy stared blankly at her. Up to that moment he had altogether forgotten that building a new cottage would mean leaving the old one. To him, the little cottage never seemed as bad as it did to the widow. He had listened, it is true, to her daily litany of its defects, but out of politeness only. Never had he seen it with her eyes, but always with his own. According to her, its tin roof was an eyesore, but he liked to hear the raindrops falling on it clear and sweet. According to her the windows were too low, and they didn't let in enough light by day, but in bed at night he could stare straight up at the stars without raising his head from the pillow. And that was a great thing surely! According to her, the cow-shed was too close to the house, but if he woke in the middle of the night, he liked to hear Bessie, the old cow, pulling at her tyings, and on cold winter nights it comforted

him to find that the fierce night air was not strong enough to kill the warm smell that came from her byre.

There was one wintry night and he thought he'd die before morning, like the poor thrushes that at times fell down out of the air, too stiff to fly, but when he thought of Bessie and the way the old cow's breath kept the byre warm, he cupped his own two hands around his mouth and breathed into them, and soon he too began to feel warm and comfortable. To him, that night, it seemed that together, he and the old cow, with their living breath were stronger than their enemies, the elements. Oh, say what you liked, a cow was great company. And as far as he was concerned, the nearer she was to the house the better. So too with many other things that the widow thought were faults in the little house; as often as not to Packy they were things in its favour. Indeed, it would want to be a wonderful place that would seem nicer and homelier to him than the cottage where he was born. After all, his mother came to it only by chance, but he came to it as a snail comes to its shell.

'Oh, Mother!' he cried, 'maybe we oughtn't to part with the old cottage till we see first if we're going to like the new one!'

To hear the sad note in his voice you'd think the day of the flitting was upon them. The widow had to laugh.

'Is that the way with you, son? You're getting sorry you made such big promises! Ah, never mind. It'll be a long time yet before you're fit to build a house for any woman, and when that time does come, I don't suppose it will be for your old mother you'll be building it.'

But her meaning was so lost on him.

'And for who else?' he cried.

But the widow turned away and as she did she caught sight of the clock.

'Look at the time! You're going to be late for school. And I have to cut your lunch yet,' she said crossly. Bustling up from the bench she seized the big cake of soda bread that she had baked and set to cool on the kitchen window-sill before he was out of bed that morning. 'Will this be enough for you?' she cried, cleaving the knife down through the bread and mortaring together two big slices with a slab of yellow butter. Then, as he stuffed the bread into his satchel and ran out of the door, she ran after him. 'Hurry home, son,' she called out, leaning far over the gate to watch him go up the road.

Hardly ever did he go out of the house that she didn't watch him out of sight, and hardly ever did he come home that she wasn't there again, waiting to get the first glimpse of him. And all the time between his going and coming, her heart was in her mouth wondering if he was safe and sound. For this reason she was often a bit edgy with him when he did come home, especially if he was a few minutes late as he was sometimes when he fell in with his friends the Tubridys.

The widow was death on the Tubridys, although nobody, least of all herself, could say why this should be so. Perhaps it was that, although she often said the whole three Tubridys – Christy and Donny and poor little Marty – all sewn up together wouldn't put a patch on her Packy, still – maybe – it annoyed her to see them trotting along behind Rose Tubridy on the way to Mass of a Sunday while she had only the one set of feet running to keep up with her.

'Well! What nonsense did the Tubridys put into your head today?' she'd call out as soon as he came within earshot.

'Oh, wait till you hear, Mother!' he'd cry, and before he got to the gate at all, he'd begin to tell all he heard that day.

One day he was very excited.

'What do you know, Mother! There is a big pot of gold buried beyond in the old abbey! Christy Tubridy is after telling me about it. He didn't know anything about it either until last night when his father told him while they were all sitting around the fire. He said he'd have got it himself long ago, only every time he put the spade into the ground, a big white cock appeared on the top of the old abbey and flapped its wings at him, and crowed three times! He had to let go the spade and run for his life! What do you think of that, Mother?'

But the widow didn't give him much hearing.

'A likely story!' she said. 'What harm would an innocent old cock have done him? Him of all people: that ought to be well used to the sound of cocks and hens, with the dungheap right under the window of the house. It's a

15

wonder he wasn't deafened long ago with cocks crowing right into his ear! Oh, it would take more than an old cock to scare that man! And furthermore, let me tell you that if there was something to be got for nothing in this world, the devil himself wouldn't knock a feather out of him till he got it. You mark my words, son, if there was as much as a farthing buried in the old abbey, by now old Tubridy would have scratched up the whole place looking for it. He wouldn't have left one stone standing on another. He'd have done a better job on it than Cromwell! A pot of gold, indeed! A likely story!'

'I suppose you're right,' said Packy, and he left down the spade that he had grabbed up to go digging for the gold.

'Don't be so ready to believe everything you hear!' said his mother.

But barely a day later he came running home again to tell something else he had heard.

'Mother! Mother! Do you know the heap of old stones at the bottom of the hill in Claddy graveyard, where there was an old church one time? Well, last night Christy Tubridy's father told him that when they were building that church long ago they never meant to build it there at all, but at the top of the hill, only the morning after they brought up the first load of stones and gravel, where did they find it all but down at the bottom of the hill! Nobody knew how it got there, but they had to spend the day bringing it all up again. And what do you suppose? The morning after when they came to work, there were all the stones and the gravel down at the bottom once more. And the same thing happened the day after that again and on every day after for seven days! But on the seventh day they knew that it must be the work of the Shee. The Shee didn't want a church built on that hill at all. There was no use going against them, so they built it down in the hollow.'

But the widow didn't give him any hearing this time either.

'A likely story!' she said. 'It's my opinion that the workmen that carried those stones up the hill by day, were the same that carried them down-hill at night. I don't suppose the men that were going in those days liked work any better than the men that are going nowadays, and it's likely they decided it would pay them better to put in a few hours overtime taking down the stones, than be lugging them up there for an eternity – as they would be in those days with not many implements. The Shee indeed! How well no one thought of sitting up one night to see who was doing the good work? Oh no. Well they knew it wasn't the Shee! But it suited them to let on to it. The Shee indeed! If that hill belongs to the Shee – which I very much doubt – what harm would it do to them to have a church built on it? Isn't it *inside* the hills the Shee live? What do they care what happens outside on the hillside? A likely story! I wonder when are you going to stop heeding those Tubridys and their nonsense?'

Never, it seemed, for the very next day he came running down the road as if he'd never get inside the gate quick enough to tell another story.

'Oh Mother!' he cried, jumping across the puddles at the door. 'Are you sure I'm yours? I mean, are you sure that I belong to you – that I'm not a changeling? Because Christy Tubridy told me that their Marty is one! I always thought he was their real brother, didn't you? Well, he's not! One day, when he was a baby, their mother was hanging out the clothes to dry on the bushes, and she had him in a basket on the ground beside her, but when she was finished hanging up the clothes she looked into the basket, and it wasn't her own baby at all that was in it but another one altogether that she'd never seen before, all wizened up, with a cute little face on him like a little old man. It was the Shee that came and stole her baby, and put the other crabby fellow in place of him. The Tubridys were terribly annoyed, but they couldn't do anything about it, and they had to rear up Marty like he was their own.'

But this time the widow gave him no hearing at all.

'A likely story!' she cried. 'A likely story indeed! Oh, isn't it remarkable the lengths people will go to make excuses for themselves. That poor child, Marty Tubridy, was never anything but a crabby thing. He's a Tubridy, all right. Isn't he the dead spit of his old grandfather that's only dead this ten years? I remember him well. So they want to let on he's a changeling? God give them wit. The Shee indeed! The Shee are no more ready than any other kind of people to do

17

themselves a bad turn, and if they make it a habit to steal human children – which I very much doubt – I'd say they'd be on the watch for some child a bit better favoured than one of those poor Tubridys. Now, if it was *you* they put their eye on, son, that would be a different matter, because – even if it's me that says it – you were the sonsiest baby anyone ever saw. Not indeed that I ever left you lying about in a basket under the bushes! It would want to be someone smart that would have stolen you! I never once took my eyes off you from the first minute I clapped them on to you, till you were big enough to look after yourself – which I suppose you are now? Or are you? Sometimes I doubt it when you come home to me stuffed with nonsense! Changeling indeed! A likely story.'

But as a matter of fact it would have been hard to find a story that would not be a likely story to the widow. The gusts of her wisdom blew so fiercely about the cottage that after a while Packy began to feel that it wasn't worth while opening his own mouth at all so quickly did his mother rend his words into rags. And when, one spring, he began to fancy every time he went out of doors that there was someone beckoning to him, and calling him by name, he said nothing at all about it to his mother. For of course he could be mistaken. It was mostly in the evenings that the fancies came to him, and the mist that rose up from the river and wandered over the fields often took odd shapes. There were even days when it never wholly lifted, and like bits of white wool torn from the backs of the sheep as they scrambled through briars and bushes, or rubbed up against barbed wire, the mist lay about the ground in unexpected hollows. It lay in the hollows that are to be found in old pasture that once was broken by the plough, and on the shallow ridges where the fallow meets the ley. Ah yes! It was easy enough then to mistake it for a white hand lifted, or a face turned for an instant towards you, and then turned swiftly aside.

It is said however that a person will get used to anything, and after a while Packy got used to his fancies. He got used to them, but he was less eager than usual to go out and wander in the fields and woods, above all after the sun went below the tops of the trees. And the widow soon noticed this. It wasn't like him to hang about the cottage after school.

What was the matter, she wondered? Did something ail him?

'Where are the Tubridys these days, son?' she asked at last. 'God knows they're here often enough when they're not wanted. It's a wonder you wouldn't like to go off with them for a ramble in the woods.'

She went to the door and looked out. It was the month of May, the very first day of it. But Packy didn't stir from the fire. Nor the next day either. Nor the next. Nor the next.

'That fire won't burn any brighter for you to be hatching it,' said the widow at last.

That was true, thought Packy, for it was a poor fire surely. He looked at it with remorse. It was nearly out. There was nothing on the hearth but a handful of twigs that were more like the makings of a jackdaw's nest than the makings of a fire. It was like a tinker's fire, no sooner kindled than crackled away in a shower of sparks. He looked at his mother. He knew what was wrong. She had no one to depend on for firing now that he never went out for he never came back without a big armful of branches from the neighbouring demesne. He looked at her hands. They were all scratched and scored from plucking the bushes.

'Oh, Mother,' he cried in true contrition, 'tomorrow on my way home from school I'll go into the woods, no matter what, and get you an armful of branches!'

But the next day – and in broad sunlight too – his fancies were worse than ever.

Just as the bell rang to call in the scholars from play, what did Packy see, around the corner of the schoolhouse, but a finger beckoning: beckoning to him! It turned out to be only the flickering of a shadow cast on the wall by an old hawthorn tree beyond the gable, but all the same it unsettled him. And when school was over he made sure to keep in the middle of the little drove of scholars that went his way home.

For there is no loneliness like the loneliness of the roads of Meath, with the big, high hedges rising up to either side of you, so that you can't even see the cattle in the fields, but only hear them inside wading in the deep grass and pulling at the brittle young briars in the hedge. Closed in between those high hedges, the road often seems endless to those who trudge along it, up hill and down, for although to the men who make ordnance maps the undulations of the land may seem no greater than the gentle undulations of the birds rising and dipping in the air above it, yet to those who go always on foot – the herd after his flock, the scholar with his satchel on his back – it has as many ripples as a sheet in the wind, and not only that, but it often seems to ripple in such a way that the rises are always in front, and the dips always behind.

It was that way with Packy anyway.

Oh, how good it would be at home: first to catch a glimpse of the little rusty roof, and then to run in at the gate and feel the splatters of the mud on his knees as he'd dash through the puddles in front of the door.

It was not till he got to Connells Cross that he remembered his promise about the fire-wood. Oh sorely, sorely was he tempted to break that promise, but after one last look at the far tin roof that had just come into view above the hedge he let the little flock of scholars go forward without him. Then, with a sad look after them he climbed up on the wall of the demesne and jumped down on the other side. Immediately, under his feet twigs and branches cracked like glass, and for a minute he was tempted to gather an armful although he knew well they were only larch and pine. But he put the base temptation from him. Try to light a fire with larch? Wasn't it larch carpenters put in the stairs of a house so the people could get down it safely if the house took fire! And pine? Wasn't it a dangerous timber always spitting out sparks that would burn holes the size of buttons in the leg of your trousers! Oh no; he'd have to do better than that; he'd have to get beech or ash or sycamore or oak. And to get them he'd have to go deep into the woods to where the trees were as old as the Christian world. He'd have to go as far as the little cemetery of Claddy. There, among the tottering tombstones and the fallen masonry of the ancient church, there was always a litter of dead branches, and what was more, every branch was crotched over with grey lichen to make it easier to see against the dark mould of the earth.

Like all cemeteries, the cemetery of Claddy was a lonely place, and to get to it he would have to cross the hill that

Christy Tubridy said belonged to Shee, but he remembered that his mother had heaped scorn on that kind of talk. All the same, when he came to the small pathway that led up to the hill, he faltered, because it was so overgrown with laurel it was more like a tunnel than a path. Away at the far end of the tunnel, though, there was a glade and there the light lay white and beautiful on the bark of the trees. Shutting his eyes, Packy dashed into the leafy tunnel and didn't open them until he was out of it. But when he did open them he had to blink, because, just as the sky would soon sparkle with stars, so, everywhere, under his feet the dark earth sparkled with white windflowers. Who could be afraid in such a place?

As for the branches: the ground was strewn with them. Ah! there was a good one! There was a fine dry one! And there was one would burn for an hour!

But it didn't pay to be too hasty. That last was a branch of blackthorn and it gave him a nasty prick – 'Ouch,' it hurt. Letting fall his bundle, Packy stuck his finger into his mouth, but the thorn had gone deep and he couldn't suck it out. He'd have to stoup his finger in hot water, or get his mother to put a poultice of bread and water on it. He'd better not forget either, he told himself, because there was poison in thorns. Christy Tubridy knew a man who... At the thought of the Tubridys, though, Packy grew uneasy. All the stories they had ever told him again crowded back into his mind. Supposing those stories were true? Supposing the Shee really did still wander about the world? Supposing they did steal away human children?

Suddenly his heart began to beat so fast it felt like it was only inside his shirt it was instead of inside his skin. And the next minute, leaving his bundle of twigs where it lay, he made for the green pathway up which he had come, meaning to fling himself down it as if it were a hole in the ground.

And that is what he would have done only that – right beside him – sitting on the stump of a tree, he caught sight of a gentleman! A stranger it is true, but a gentleman. At least, Packy took him to be that – a gentleman from the Big House, perhaps? Now, although Packy was glad he was not alone, he was afraid the gentleman might be cross with him

for trespassing. But not at all. The gentleman was very affable.

'There's a fine dry limb of a tree!' he said, pointing to a bough of ash that Packy had overlooked.

He spoke so civilly that Packy ventured a close look at him.

Was he a man at all, he wondered? The clothes on him were as fine as silk, and a most surprising colour: green. As for his shoes, they were so fine his muscles rippled under the leather like the muscles of a finely bred horse ripple under his skin. There was something a bit odd about him.

'Thank you, sir,' said Packy cautiously and he bent and picked up the branch.

'Don't mention it: I assure you it's a pleasure to assist you, Packy.' In surprise Packy stared. The gentleman knew his name!

'Yes, Packy, I know your name – and all about you,' said the little gentleman smiling. 'In fact I have been endeavouring all the week to have a word with you – alone, that is to say – but I found it impossible to attract your attention – until now!'

Packy started. So he wasn't mistaken after all when he fancied that someone was beckoning to him, and raising a hand.

'Was it you, sir?' he cried in amazement. 'I thought it was only the mist. Tell me, sir – were you at it again today?' he cried. The little gentleman nodded. 'Well doesn't that beat all!' said Packy. 'I thought it was a branch of hawthorn swaying in the wind.'

The gentleman bowed.

'I'm complimented. A beautiful tree; always a favourite of mine, especially a long bush of it in the middle of a green field. But to come to practical matters. I suppose you're wondering what I wanted to see you about. Well, let me tell you straight away – I understand that you are dissatisfied with the condition of your cottage – is that so?'

He was a County Councillor! That was it! – thought Packy. He'd come to make a report on the condition of the cottage. And to think he had nearly run away from him!

'It's in a very bad state, sir,' he said. 'My mother is very anxious to get out of it.'

To a County Councillor that ought to be broad enough! Better however leave nothing to chance. 'Perhaps there is something you could do for us, sir,' he said. Throwing down his bundle of kindling he went nearer. What were a few bits of rotten branch to compare with the news he'd be bringing home if the gentleman promised him a Council cottage?

'Well, Packy, perhaps there may be something I can do for you!' said the gentleman. 'Sit down here beside me, and we'll discuss the matter, or better still, let us walk up and down; it gets so chilly out on the hillside at this hour of evening.'

And indeed it was more than chilly. The mist had started to rise. Already it roped the boles of the trees, and if it weren't for the little gentleman's company Packy would have been scared. As it was, he set about matching his pace to the pace of his friend, and stepped out boldly.

'I suppose you're a County Councillor, sir?' he asked, as they paced along.

'Eh? A County Councillor? What's that?' said the little man, and he stopped short in his stride, but the next minute he started off again. 'Don't let us delay,' he said. 'It's mortally cold out here.'

So he wasn't a County Councillor? He didn't even know what a Councillor was! Packy's heart sank. Where did he come from at all? And was it all for nothing he'd lost his time and his firewood. It was very tiring too, striding up and down on the top of the hill, because at every minute the little gentleman stepped out faster and faster, and where at first, when they passed them, the windflowers had shone out each single as a star, now they streamed past like ribbons of mist. Even the little man was out of breath. He was panting like the pinkeens that Packy and the Tubridys caught in the Boyne and put into jam-jars where they swam to the sides of the glass, their mouths gaping. Chancing to glance at him it seemed to Packy that the little man had got a lot older looking. His eyes looked very old!

'What's the matter, Packy?' asked the little man, just then, seeing him stare.

'Nothing, sir,' said Packy – 'I was just wondering if it is a thing that you are a foreigner?'

'Is it me?' cried the gentleman, 'a foreigner!' He stopped short in astonishment. 'I've been in this country a lot longer than you, Packy!' He paused, '– about five thousand years longer, I should say.'

Packy too stopped short.

Was the little man cracked, he wondered? This, however, was a point he could not very well ask the gentleman to settle. He would have to decide for himself. So he said nothing. But he wasn't going to pace up and down the hill any more.

'I think I'd better be going home, sir,' he said politely, but decisively.

'Oh, but you can't go back to that wretched cottage,' cried the gentleman. 'Not till I see if I can do something for you!' he cried. 'Have you forgotten?'

Of course he hadn't forgotten. But if the gentleman was cracked, what use was there placing any hope in him?

'I've been thinking of your problem for some time past, Packy, as it happens,' he said, 'and it seems to me that there is very little use in trying to do anything to that old place of yours–'

That was sane enough, thought Packy.

'– and so,' he went on, 'what I have in mind is that you come and live with *me*!'

So he *was* cracked after all! Packy drew back. But the little man went on eagerly. 'I live right near here – yes – just down there – only a few paces,' he cried, pointing down the side of the hill towards the water's edge.

Now Packy wouldn't swear that he knew every single step of the ground at this point, because a great deal of it was covered with briar and scrub, but he'd be prepared to swear that there wasn't a house the size of a sixpence on the side of that hill!

'I see you don't believe me!' said the little man. 'Well – come and I'll show you!'

Now, the little man was so insistent, and Packy himself was so curious, that when the former set off down the slope, Packy set off after him, although it was by no means easy to follow him, for the undergrowth was dense, and the branches of the trees, that had never been cut back, or broken by cattle, hung down so low that in some places they touched the ground. To pass under them Packy had almost to go down on his knees. But the little fellow knew his way like a rabbit. He looped under the heavy boughs as easily as a bird, while Packy stumbled after, as often as not forgetting to lower his head, and getting a crack on the pate. 'Ouch!' he cried on one of these occasions.

'What's up?' asked the little man, looking irritably over his shoulder.

'I hit my head against a branch; that's all,' said Packy.

The little man looked crossly at him.

'That wasn't a branch you hit against,' he said sharply, 'it was a root!'

And indeed he was right. At that point, the hill sloped so steeply that the rain had washed the clay from the roots of the trees till you could walk under them in the same way as you'd walk through the eye of a bridge. It was just as he was about to duck under another of these big branching roots after the little man, that Packy noticed how dark it was on the other side, as if something had come up between them and the sky. He came to an abrupt stand. The little man, on the other hand, darted into the dimness.

'Mind your step there,' he cried, looking back over his shoulder. 'It's a bit dark, but you'll get used to it.' He fully expected Packy to follow him.

But Packy stuck his feet in the ground.

'Hold on a minute, sir,' he said. 'If it's a cave you live in, I'm not going a step further.

He hadn't forgotten how, once, an uncle of his had come home from America, and hired a car and took him and his mother to New Grange to see the prehistoric caves. His mother couldn't be got to go into them, but he and his uncle crawled down a stone passage that was slimy and wet, and when they got to the caves they hardly had room to stand up. They could barely breathe either the air was so damp. And it had a smell like the smell that rises from a newly-made grave. All the time Packy kept thinking the earth would press down on the cave and crack it like an egg – and them along with it. No thank you! He had seen enough caves!

'You're not going to get me into any cave,' he said stoutly. The little man ran out into the light again.

'It's not a cave!' he cried. 'Do you think we had to scratch holes for ourselves like badgers or foxes? We may live inside the hill but we move around under the earth the same way that you move around over it. You've a lot to learn yet, Packy, you and your generation.'

'Is that so?' said Packy. 'Well, we can move in the air! And under the sea!'

'Bah!' said the little man. 'Not the way I meant! Not like the birds! Not like the fishes!'

'I suppose you're right there,' said Packy, but half-heartedly.

'What do you mean by supposing everything?' said the old man crossly. 'Don't you ever say yes or no? I hope you haven't a suspicious streak in you? Perhaps I should have known that when you kept running home all week every time I tried to get your attention!'

'Oh, but that was different, sir,' said Packy. 'I thought then that you were one of the Shee!'

At this, however, the little man began to laugh.

'And who in the name of the Sod do you think I am *now*?' he said.

'I don't know, sir,' said Packy, 'but I'm not afraid of you anyway – a nice kind gentleman like you – why should I?'

'And if I were to tell you that I *am* one of the Shee,' said the little man, 'what would happen then?'

Packy pondered this.

'Perhaps you'd be only joking?' he said, but a doubtful look had come on his face.

'And if I wasn't joking,' said the little man, 'what then?'

'Well, sir,' said Packy, 'I suppose I'd be twice as glad then that I didn't go into the cave with you!'

'I tell you it's *not* a cave!' screamed the little man. 'And by the same token, will you stop calling us the Shee! What do they teach you in school at all, at all? Did you never hear tell of the Tuatha de Danaan? the noblest race that ever set foot in this isle? In five thousand years, no race has equalled us in skill or knowledge.'

Five thousand years! Packy started. Had he heard aright?

'Excuse me, sir,' he said then. 'Are you alive or dead?'

It seemed quite a natural question to ask, but it angered the little man.

28

'Do I look as if I was dead?' he cried. 'Wouldn't I be dust and ashes long ago if so?'

'Oh, I don't know about that,' said Packy. 'When my uncle hired the car that time – the time we went to New Grange –we passed through Drogheda, and we went to the Cathedral to see Blessed Oliver Plunkett's head. It's in a box on the altar. He's dead hundreds of years: and he's not dust and ashes!'

But truth to tell, there was a big difference between the little gentleman's head, and the head of the saint, because the venerable bishop's head looked like an old football, nothing more, while the little gentleman looked very much alive, especially at that moment, because he was leaping with anger.

'Are you taught nothing at all nowadays?' he cried in disgust. 'Do you not know anything about the history of your country? Were you not taught that when we went into the hills we took with us the secret that mankind has been seeking ever since – the secret of eternal youth? But come! that's not the point. The point is – are you coming any further, or are you not?'

Now there was no doubt about it, the situation had changed. Packy stared past the little man, and although he could see nothing, his curiosity undecided him. What a story he'd have for the Tubridys if he'd once been inside that hill!

'Will you bring me back again, sir?' he asked, having in mind the story about the changelings.

The little man looked at him.

'Well, Packy, I may as well be straight with you. An odd time – now and again only – we take a notion for a human child and try to lure him away to live with us forever under the hills, but we always look for one who is dissatisfied with his lot in the world.'

'Oh, but I'm not dissatisfied with my lot,' cried Packy apprehensively.

'Oh come now!' said the little man, 'didn't I often overhear you and your mother complaining about that wretched cottage of yours?'

'Oh, you might have heard us talking, sir, but it was my mother that was discontented: not me. I was only agreeing to keep her in good humour.'

'What's that?' said the little man sharply. 'Don't tell me I've got the wrong end of the stick! Are you sure of what you're saying, Packy? Because if that's the case I may as well stop wasting my time.' He scowled very fiercely. After a minute though he seemed to remember his manners. 'It's too bad,' he said, 'because you're the sort of lad I like.'

'Thank you, sir,' said Packy. 'My mother will be pleased to hear that.' Then as he made a move to go, upon an impulse he stopped. 'I wonder, sir, if you'd mind my asking you a question before I go?'

'Why certainly not,' said the little man. 'But be quick, boy; it's very cold out here on the hillside.'

'Well, sir,' said Packy, 'I'd like to know if it's true about Marty Tubridy – I mean – is he a changeling, sir?'

'Is it Marty Tubridy! Of course not!' said the old man. 'Your mother was right there,' he conceded. 'We have no use for weedy little creatures like the Tubridys: it isn't everyone we fancy, I can tell you.'

That was very gratifying to hear. His mother would be pleased at that too, thought Packy. Then he remembered that she would probably say it was all a likely story. He sighed.

The little man looked keenly at him.

'Are you changing your mind?'

Packy said nothing for a minute. Then he looked up.

'You didn't tell me whether I'd be able to get out again?' he asked.

'Really, Packy, you are an obstinate boy! I have no choice but to tell you the truth, which is that at the start I had no notion of letting you out again if I once got you inside, but as it's getting late, and I'm getting sick and tired arguing, I'm willing to make a bargain with you. I won't stop you from going home – if you want to go yourself, but don't blame me if you don't want to go!'

Well, that seemed fair enough.

'Oh, there's no fear of me wanting to stay!' he said confidently. 'Thank you kindly for asking me, sir. I'll go on for a short while. But wait a second while I take off my boots so I won't dirty the place: my feet are shocking muddy after slithering down that slope.'

For a minute the little gentleman looked oddly at him.

'Leave on your boots, Packy,' he said; then slowly and solemnly: 'Don't leave anything belonging to you outside. That's the very thing I'd have made you do, if I was not going to let you out again. I'd have had you leave some part of your clothing – your cap, or your scarf, or something, here on the outside of the hill – like a man would leave his clothes on the bank of the river if he was going to drown himself – so that people would find them and give up hopes of you. Because as long as there's anyone outside in the world still hoping a child will come back to them, it's nearly as hard for us to keep him inside as if he himself was still hoping to go back. Keep your boots on your feet, boy. You can't say I'm not being honest with you, can you?'

'I cannot, sir,' said Packy, 'but tell me, sir, those children you were telling me about – the ones that didn't want to go back to the world, did they always leave their shoes outside?'

'They did,' said the little man.

'Did they now?' said Packy reflectively. 'Wasn't that very foolish of them? How did they know they wouldn't be sorry when they got inside?'

The little man shrugged his shoulders.

'Ah sure don't we all have to take a chance some time or another in our lives?' he said. 'Look at us! Before we came to Erin we were endlessly sailing the seas looking for a land to our liking. And many a one we found. But it never satisfied us for long. No matter how often be beached our boats, we soon set sail again, till one day we saw *this* island rise up out of the seas and we put all our trust in the promise of her emerald shores. Before we went a foot inland do you know what we did? We set fire to our boats, down on the grey sands! That was taking a chance, wasn't it? So you can't expect me to have much sympathy with people that won't take a chance with their boots! Have you made up your mind about yours, by the way? You won't leave them? Very well then, lace them up again on you, and don't mind them being muddy. I'll get one of the women inside to give them a rub of a blacking brush. They're very muddy all right. Never mind that now though – follow me!' Then he turned around and ducking under the root of the tree again, he walked into what seemed to Packy to be a solid wall of earth.

But just as fog shrinks from light, or frost from fire, so, as they went inward, the earth seemed to give way before them. Nor was it the cold wet rock of New Grange either, but a warm dry clay in which, Packy noticed with interest as they went along, there were different layers of clay and sand and gravel and stone, just like he had seen in Swainstown Quarry when he went there once on a tipper-lorry. In fact he was so interested in the walls of clay that he hardly realized how deep into the hill they were going until the little man came to a stop.

'Well! Here we are!' he said, and Packy saw that they had arrived at what at first seemed to be a large room, but which he soon saw was merely a large space made by several people all gathered together.

But apparently these people rarely moved very far from where they were, for around them they had collected a variety of articles that suggested permanent habitation, in the way that furniture suggests habitaton in a house. Not that the articles in the cave were furniture in any real sense of the word. Tables and chairs there were none. But in a corner a big harp gleamed, and randomly around about were strewn a number of vessels, basins and ewers and yes, a row of gleaming milking pails! With astonishment, Packy noticed that all these vessels, and the harp too, were as bright as if they were made of gold! He was staring at them when the little man shook him by the arm.

'Well, how do you like it down here?' he cried, and he was so feverishly excited he was dancing about on the tips of his toes.

Now, Packy didn't want to be rude, but the fact of the matter was that only for the gold basins and the gold pails and the big gold harp, he didn't see anything very wonderful about the place. But of course, they would be something to tell the Tubridys about.

'They're not real gold, sure they're not?' he asked.

'Of course they are gold,' said the little man. And then, seeing that Packy seemed to doubt him, he frowned. 'In our day Ireland was the Eldorado of the world. I thought everyone knew that! Everything was made of gold. Even our buttons. Even the latchets of our shoes!' And he held out his foot to show that, sure enough, although Packy hadn't noticed it before, the latchets were solid gold. 'It was a good job for us that gold was plentiful,' he said irritably. 'I don't know what we'd do if we had to put up with some of the utensils you have today.'

'Oh, they're not too bad,' said Packy. 'There are grand enamel pails and basins in Leonards of Trim!'

'Is that so?' said the little man coldly. 'Perhaps it's a matter of taste. To be candid with you though, Packy, I wouldn't like to have to spend five thousand years looking at some of the delph on your kitchen-dresser!'

Packy laughed. 'There'd be no fear you'd have to look that long at them,' he said. 'They don't last any time. They's always getting broken.'

'Ah, that's not the way in here,' said the little man. 'Nothing ever gets cracked down here; nothing ever gets broken.'

Packy stared. 'You don't tell me!' he said. 'Do you never knock the handle off a cup, or a jug?' That was a thing he was always doing.

The little man shook his head.

'Oh, but I forgot,' said Packy, 'gold wouldn't break so easily.' Not that he thought it was such a good idea to have cups made of gold. When you'd pour your tea into them, wouldn't it get so hot it would scald the lip off you?

One day in the summer that was gone past, he and the Tubridys went fishing on the Boyne up beyond Rathnally, and they took a few grains of tea with them in case they got dry. They forgot to bring cups though, and they had to empty their tin-cans of worms and use them for cups. But the metal rim of the can got red hot the minute the tea went into it, and they couldn't drink a drop. Gold would be just the same?

But in fact, there were no cups at all, it appeared.

'One no longer has any need for food, Packy,' said the little man, 'once one has learned the secret of eternal youth!'

'Do you mean you don't eat anything?' cried Packy, 'anything at all? Don't you ever feel hungry?'

'No, child,' said the little man sedately. 'Desire withers when perfection flowers. And if you stay here with us for long, you'll lose all desire too.'

'You're joking, sir!' said Packy, doubtful. At that very minute he had a powerful longing for a cut of bread and a swig of milk. Indeed he glanced involuntarily at the gold milking pails. The Tubridys said the Shee often stole into byres and stripped the cows' udders.

The little man had seen his glance and must have read his thoughts.

'A little harmless fun now and then,' he said, shamefacedly.

Had they been stripping cows lately? Packy wondered. Perhaps there might be a dreg in the bottom of one of the buckets? He craned his neck to see them. They were all empty!

'I'm very dry, sir,' he said.

'That's only your imagination,' said the little man crossly. 'Stand there for a minute, like a good boy,' he said then and he darted over to one of the women. 'There's something wrong somewhere,' he said to a woman that was sitting by the harp. And then he snapped his fingers. 'It's the boots,' he cried.

The young woman stood up. 'Give me your boots, son,' she said, 'and I'll get the mud off them.'

Now Packy was always shy of strange women, but this one spoke so like Mrs Tubridy that he felt at home with her at once. And indeed, just as Mrs Tubridy would have done, she caught the sleeve of his coat in her two fists and began to rub off the mud that was caked on it. It didn't brush off so easily though.

'I'll have to take a brush to it,' she said. 'Take your coat off, son, and I'll give it a rub too when I'm doing your boots.'

'That's very kind of you, ma'am,' said Packy, and he took off his coat. It was the coat of his good suit. His mother made him wear it that day so she'd get a chance to put a patch on the elbow of his old one. His vest was the vest belonging to the old suit.

'Is there mud on your vest as well?' asked the young woman.

'Oh no, ma'am,' said Packy. 'That's only splatters of pig-food and chicken-mash.'

34

'What matter! Give it to me,' she said. 'I may as well make the one job of it.'

But when he took off his vest his shirt was a show.

'That's only sweat-marks,' he protested, knowing she'd proffer to do the shirt as well. But there was no holding back from her any more than from his mother.

'Here, sonny,' she cried. 'Go behind that harp over there and take every stitch off you and we'll get them all cleaned and pressed for you. You can put this on while you're waiting,' she said, and she whipped a green dust-sheet off another harp.

It seemed to Packy that such courtesy was hardly necessary, but he went obediently behind the harp and stripped to the skin. Just as he reached out his hand, however, for the dust-sheet, the young woman came back with a big gold basin of water.

'What's that for?' cried Packy, drawing away from her.

She shoved a towel into his hands.

'Wrap that towel around you,' she said, 'while I try to get some of the dirt off you before you get back into your clean clothes.'

'Mud isn't dirt!' cried Packy indignantly. 'My mother washes me every Saturday night,' he cried, 'and this is only Tuesday.'

At this point the little man hurried over to them.

'It's not a question of cleanliness, Packy,' he said. 'It's a question of hospitality. Surely the ancient customs of the Gael have not fallen into such disuse in Ireland today? Does your mother not offer ablutions to those who cross your threshold?'

'What's that, sir?' said Packy, but he recollected that one day when his teacher called at the cottage, he slipped on the spud-stone at the gate and fell into a puddle, and that day his mother ran into the house and got out a big enamel basin and filled it with water for him to wash his hands. Then she got a towel and wiped the mud off the tail of his coat. She offered him an old pair of his father's pants too, but he wouldn't put them on. Oh, his mother wasn't far behind anyone, he thought, when it came to hospitality. And so, to show that he was very familiar with all such rites, he made an opening in the towel, and unbared first one hand, and then the other.

'That's a good boy,' she said. 'Now your foot. Now the other one!'

She didn't stop at his feet though, and before he knew where he was, there wasn't a cranny of him she hadn't scrubbed.

Never in his life had he been washed like that. It reminded him of the way Mrs Tubridy scoured old grandpa Tubridy's corpse the night he was waked.

He was especially struck with the way the black rims of his nails stood out against his bone-white hands. And he greatly regretted it when the young woman prised out the dirt with a little gold pin. And when she was done with his finger-nails, she began to prod at his toe-nails!

They must be terrible clean people altogether, he thought. His own mother was supposed to be the cleanest woman in the parish, yet she'd never dream of going that far. When his father died, and she was describing the kind of mortuary card she wanted to get for him, she held up her hand to the shopkeeper and showed him the rim of dirt under her nail.

'I want the border of the card as deep as that!' she said. Indeed she'd speak of the black of her nail as readily as another person would speak of the white of his eye!

These people must be terrible particular people, he thought. All those gold basins and gold ewers were for washing themselves, he supposed. And just then the young woman took out a comb and began to rake his hair so hard he felt as if he'd been sculled. But the comb was solid gold too.

'Oh wait till the Tubridys hear about this,' he said ecstatically.

The young woman looked at him in a very peculiar way, and then she looked at the little man.

'There's something wrong still,' said the little man.

'Are you sure you washed every nook of him?' he asked. He'd got very cross again.

'I did,' said the young woman, and she was cross too.

I hope they're not going to start fighting, while I'm standing here in my skin, thought Packy, and he shivered. He ventured to pluck the little man by the sleeve.

36

'Excuse me, sir,' he said as politely as possible. 'Are my own clothes near ready do you think?'

But these innocent words seemed to infuriate the little man, and he turned on the young woman again.

'You missed some part of him!' he shouted. 'What about his ears? Did you take the wax out of them?'

'Oh, I forgot,' cried the young woman, and whipping the gold pin out of her bodice again she began to root in his ears.

There was such a lot of wax in his ears, Packy was shamed and he thought he'd better pass it off with a joke.

'I'll have no excuse now but to get up when my mother calls me in the morning,' he said.

But the little man seemed ready to dance with rage at that. 'What about his teeth?' he cried, ignoring him and calling to the young woman. 'Maybe there's a bit of food stuck between them?'

'That's it surely!' cried the young woman. 'Open your mouth, Packy,' she said, and she began to poke between his teeth with the needle, but to no avail. There was not a thing between his bright white teeth.

He had to laugh. 'That's the way the vet opens Bessie's mouth,' he said. 'Bessie is our cow.'

'Bother your cow Bessie,' said the little man, and he caught the young woman by the arm and shook her. 'Could there be a bit of grit in his eye?'

'I don't think so,' said the young woman, 'but we can try!' and she reached out and pushed up his eyelid. 'Nothing there,' she said. Then she looked into his other eye. 'Nothing there either.'

What was all this about? Packy wondered. What were they looking to find? And what about the milk? He thought they were going to try to get him a cup of milk after they'd washed him. He was still thirsty. But it was hardly worth while troubling them to get it for him, because he'd have to be going home. It would be getting very dark in the woods outside, he thought, and he looked around.

'Have you no windows?' he cried.

'What would we want with windows!' the little man exclaimed. 'If some people like to wake up and find the quilt all wet with rain, there are other people who don't,' he said venomously.

'Oh, but it isn't always raining!' cried Packy, knowing it was his own little window at home to which the little man was referring. And thinking of that small square window on a sunny morning his face lit up. There was something to be said for a broken pane at times. 'Once a swallow flew in my window – through the hole in the glass,' he said, and he gave a laugh of delight at the memory of it.

But the young woman made a face.

'Don't talk about birds!' she said. 'Dirty little things, always letting their droppings fall on everything.'

'It's great manure, though,' cried Packy. 'If you could get enough of it, you could make your fortune selling it to the people in the towns.'

At this however the little man shuddered violently.

'We may at times have vague regrets for the world outside, Packy,' he said in an admonitory tone, 'regrets for the stars, and the flowers, and the soft summer breezes, but we are certainly not sorry to have said farewell to the grosser side of life to which you have just now – somewhat indelicately – alluded.'

Packy stared, and there was a puzzled look on his face but suddenly it cleared and he nodded his head sagaciously. 'I suppose you were born in the town, sir?' he said. 'My mother says when people from the towns come out for a day in the country, they never stop talking about the smell of the flowers and the smell of the hay, but give them one smell of a cow-shed and they're ready to run back to the town. But it's not a bad smell at all when you're used to it. I suppose it makes a difference too when you have a cow of your own; like us. I love the smell of the dung in Bessie's byre!'

'Indeed?' said the little man. 'You don't tell me!' He must have been sarcastic though, because he turned to the young woman. 'That's the limit!' he said. 'I think we may give him up as a bad job.' He turned back to Packy. 'Do you still feel the need of a cup of milk?'

'If it's not too much trouble, sir, please,' said Packy.

'I didn't say you were going to get it,' said the little man testily. 'I asked if you felt the need of it.'

'I do, sir,' said Packy, 'but perhaps it's not worth bothering you. I ought to be thinking of getting home.

38

'Did you hear that?' the little man cried, fairly screeching, as he turned to the young woman. 'Oh, there is no doubt about it, there is something wrong somewhere. We'd better let him go home.'

The young woman looked very sour. 'The sooner the better, if you ask me,' she said. 'What kind of child is he at all? Why didn't you pick an ordinary one?'

'But he *is* an ordinary child,' screamed the little man. It's not my fault, and it's certainly not his!' He turned to Packy. 'Don't mind her, Packy. Women are all the same, under the hills, or over the hills. You may as well go home. And you'd be advised to start off soon, because it will be dark out on the hillside. Wait a minute till I get your clothes!'

When they got his clothes, Packy couldn't help noticing that the mud was still on them. And his boots were still in a shocking state.

'Tch, tch, tch!' said the little man. 'Women again! Try to overlook it, Packy, as a favour to me. – Well? Are you ready? Better take my hand: it's always easier to get in here than it is to get out!'

Yet a second later Packy saw a chink of light ahead, and it widened and widened until suddenly he was at the opening of the hill again, and above him was a great expanse of moonlit sky.

'I'm afraid there was a shower while we were inside,' said the little man. 'I hope your twigs didn't get wet!'

'Oh, I may leave them till morning anyway,' said Packy. He had been wondering how he'd carry them the way his finger had begun to throb with the pain of the thorn in it.

'And why would you do that?' said the little man. 'Won't your mother want them first thing in the morning?'

'She will,' said Packy, '– but my finger is beginning to beal, I'm afraid,' and he stuck it into his mouth again.

'What is the matter with it?' cried the little man. 'Show me!'

'Oh, it's nothing, sir,' said Packy. 'Only an old thorn I got when I snatched up a bit of blackthorn.'

But the little man was beside himself.

'Show me! Show me!' he screeched. 'A thorn!' and he caught Packy's hand and tried to peer at it, but the moon had gone behind a cloud. He stamped his foot angrily. 'You don't mean to tell me it was there all the time! Oh, weren't we blind! It was *that* thorn kept pulling your mind back to the world. Oh, how was it we didn't see it?'

'How could you see it, sir?' said Packy. 'It's gone in deep. It'll have to have a poultice put on it.'

At that moment the moon sailed into a clearing in the clouds and shone down bright. The little man caught him by the sleeve.

'Will you come back for a minute and we'll take it out for you?' he cried. 'There's nothing safer than a gold pin when probing for a thorn.'

Packy held back. The little man meant well, he supposed, but God help him if he was depending on that same young woman who was supposed to have polished his boots and brushed his suit.

'I'd better go home and get my mother to do it,' he said.

The little man let go of his sleeve.

'All right, Packy,' he said. 'Go home to your mother. I can't blame you. I suppose you see through the whole thing anyway! As long as there was any particle of the earth still on you, you'd never lose your hankering for home. But I hope those women didn't handle you too roughly.'

'Oh not at all, sir,' said Packy politely.

His mother wouldn't have to wash him again for a year of Saturdays.

'Well I'm glad to think you bear no ill will,' said the little man. 'I wouldn't like you to have any hard feelings towards us.' Then he shook his head sadly. 'You must admit it was a bit unfortunate for me to be bested by a bit of a thorn. Ah well, it can't be helped now.'

He looked so sad Packy felt sad too.

'I suppose I'll see you around the woods some time, sir,' he said.

But the little man shook his head from side to side.

'I don't think you will,' he said.

There seemed no more to say.

'Well, I suppose I'd better be going,' said Packy. 'I hope I'll find my way.'

'Oh, you'll find your way all right,' said the little man. 'The moon is a fine big May moon. I'm sorry about your boots,' he added, calling after him, but he couldn't resist a last sly dig. 'Anyway you'd only destroy them again going in through the puddles around your door!'

'Oh, I don't mind the puddles,' said Packy. 'Only for the puddles we couldn't keep ducks; they'd be always straying down to the Boyne, and in the end they'd swim away from us altogether. Puddles have their uses.'

At that the little man laughed.

'I never met the like of you, Packy!' he said. 'Good- bye!'

'Good-bye sir,' said Packy.

And then he was alone.

Slowly he started up the hill until he came to the top where the windflowers were all closed up for the night. But on their shiny leaves the moon lay white. And there, a dark patch in the middle of the glade, was his bundle of twigs.

He gathered them up. His finger was still throbbing but he paid no heed to the pain. Only for that thorn he might never have got out of the cave. Because it wasn't much better than a cave, no matter what the little man said about it. He began to whistle. And when he came to the pathway leading to the gap in the demesne wall he ran down it full-tilt. In a minute he was out on the road again.

There had been a shower all right. All along the road there were puddles. But in every puddle there was a star. And when he got to the cottage the puddles around the door were as big as ever, but in them shone the whole glory of the heavens.

'Is that you, Packy?' cried the widow, running out to the door in a terrible state. 'What kept you so late, son?'

'Oh, wait till I tell you,' cried Packy, although he knew right well what she'd say:

A likely story!

Janet McNeill (1907-   )
Janet McNeill was born in Dublin on 14 September 1907, and was
educated in England before beginning work as a journalist on *The Belfast
Telegraph*. She wrote many short stories and novels as well as a great
number of children's books. She has a rare gift for making very simple
stories funny and sympathetic, and she created one of her most lovable
characters in Specs MacCann. In 'The Breadth of a Whisker' she
presents a multi-layered story which can be read quite simply as a tale of
a little mouse and his magician friend or as a comment on the lust for
materialistic things.

The Breadth of a Whisker
Janet McNeill

THIS WAS THE TIME that the alchemist loved best. There was
no sound anywhere in the house, and the dark quiet rooms
lay round him like a spell. Sometimes the goldfinch in its
wicker cage at the window stirred and slept again. He heard
the little flame licking the bottom of the crucible. The liquid
in it seethed and steamed, and released a large single bubble
that swelled on its surface and reflected the solitary lamp by
which he worked before it burst, with a soft plopping noise,
and another bubble rose to take its place.

During the daytime the alchemist was busy with salves
and potions and draughts and unguents, for children with
bruised knees and young girls with broken hearts and
noblemen with black melancholy and old people with the
rheumatics; but the night – the night was all his own.

Not quite his own; it was so still that he heard the small
brown mouse as he scuttered from his mouse-hole in the
wainscot and came across the floor like a shadow, and sat
down at his feet.

'You're late,' he said, without turning to look round. He
was adding single drops of rose-red liquid from a phial into
the crucible. As they fell, one by one, they filled the air with
perfume, like a hedge of summer honeysuckle.

'Maybe I am late,' the mouse said, panting from his

42

exertion, 'but if there were more crumbs from your supper table in the evening, I wouldn't have to look so far afield to feed my family.'

The alchemist sighed. 'I daresay,' he agreed, 'but some day – some day – there will be plenty of crumbs,' and he bent over the liquid again.

The mouse's eyes shone and he pricked up his whiskers. 'Tonight? Do you think it will be tonight?'

'It could be any night,' the alchemist told him, watching how one bubble more huge than the others had risen, sleek as steel, and with every colour from the rainbow streaking its arching sides. The mouse watched it too, and neither of them spoke until it burst. Then the little animal shook his furry face dry from the explosion.

'That's what I tell my wife when she grumbles,' he said, '*any* night, I say. And I must be there on the night when it happens.'

'I know,' said the alchemist. He told his wife the same thing. She was asleep upstairs with her golden hair spread out on the pillow and the gold wedding-ring round her finger.

The sand in the hour-glass had almost run out. As the last of the grains hurried through – it was so quiet that the alchemist fancied he heard them rubbing and grinding together in their haste – he leaned forward and with a finger and thumb outstretched he dropped into the crucible a pinch of small crystals as bright as purple violets. They fell with a hiss and a stinging green steam rose from the liquid and filled the room.

'I like that one,' the mouse said when he had stopped coughing. 'I shall tell the children about it in the morning. Has anything happened?'

The alchemist wiped his streaming eyes with the long pointed sleeve of his jacket. The liquid in the crucible was now the colour of a jay's wing feathers and ran in a small whirling tide restlessly round the vessel's lip.

'No,' he said, unable to hide the disappointment from his voice, 'nothing.'

'But what a beautiful colour it is, even if it isn't the one you had hoped it would be!'

The alchemist turned the pages of his great tattered book. He lifted a quill pen and wrote in it, adorning each letter with careful flourishes. The pen squeaked and the goldfinch turned round on its perch.

The alchemist lifted a handful of flowers with spotted outthrust tongues. 'You're a good friend,' he said to the mouse, 'and if there's ever anything I can do for you –'

'There is just one thing,' the mouse told him, and his black nose-tip was lively with nervous excitement.

'Well, what is it?'

'On the night when it happens – and I shall be here, mind you, to see it happen – may I – would it be too much to ask that I – could you allow me to – just to dip one whisker into it – oh, not very deep – so that I may show it to my wife and family when I go down into my mouse-hole in the morning?'

The little animal stopped, panting. The alchemist was plucking the spotted tongues out of the flowers. When he had done this he put them into his mortar and ground them with a pestle.

'Very well,' he said, 'it's a promise. You're very sure, aren't you, that it will happen? After all these nights, you are still sure?'

'Oh yes,' said the mouse, 'aren't you?'

The alchemist didn't answer. From the bruised tongues of the flowers he had extracted a drop of liquid that he gathered in the bowl of a spoon. Although the tongues were purple the liquid was white and milky, like a pearl. The alchemist held the spoon over the crucible and tilted it, and the pearl fell in and was swallowed up.

As it fell they heard the sound of a deep note, like the single stroke of a bell. The whole room became dark, even the lamp went out, and the little flame below the crucible grew pale and lay flat.

The mouse cried out in terror and he ran and hid in the alchemist's sleeve, and they waited.

Something in the crucible was shining, faintly at first, but always increasing until it grew and grew and filled the room to its furthest corner with brilliant yellow light. Then it flashed and darkened, and there was no light at all except from some small particle that lay in the bottom of the crucible, a mere trace, a grain, a drop, something bright, something – golden!

With shaking hands the alchemist lit the lamp and bent to look. The mouse crept from his sleeve. Yes, it was there, a bright bead, lying at the bottom of the crucible.

'Gold!' said the alchemist. 'Gold, gold, gold!'

They stared at it together.

The mouse was the first to find his tongue. He ran round and round on the stone floor, jabbering with excitement.

'You've done it! – I knew you'd do it! – I always told my wife you would! – you're famous! – no one has done it before! – no more stale breadcrumbs now! – no more rinds of mouldy cheese! – fresh moist yellow cake crumbs! – mountains of them! – and a rasher of smoky bacon for the asking! – and you famous! – the whole house full of gold! – nothing all day to do! – and a golden ring on every finger of your wife's two hands! – and every feather of the goldfinch gold! – and his cage gold! – and nothing to do at night but sleep! – on a bed of gold! – go on now and wake your wife – tell her – what are you waiting for?'

The alchemist rose and went up the stairs. The goldfinch opened a sleepy eye at him as he passed the cage and thrust its head deeper into the shadow of its gold-barred wing. In the room aloft his wife was sleeping deeply. How thin the little ring of gold was that lay on her finger! He lifted a braid of her hair, wondering if it was as bright as the gold in the crucible. And then, without waking her, he came downstairs again to his workroom.

The mouse was still where he had left him, staring at the bead of gold with round dark eyes that reflected it, like the golden heads of twin pins.

'Did you not tell her?' he said over his shoulder, 'what are you waiting for?'

'What are you waiting for yourself?' asked the alchemist, 'there's nothing more to keep you here.'

The fact grew slowly in the little beast's mind. Excitement and pleasure ebbed. His whiskers drooped. Then the alchemist remembered. He lifted the crucible off the flame and held it out. 'There isn't very much of it,' he said, 'best go ahead before it cools.'

The mouse trembled from nose-tip to tail-tip. 'Do you mean it?' he asked.

'Wasn't it a promise?'

The mouse jumped on to the alchemist's arm. On small excited feet he went up the alchemist's wrist, out along his palm, down his long thumb, and there he stopped at the rim of the crucible and gently, so very gently, he tilted his head and dipped one whisker down.

46

When he lifted it again the whisker tip was gilded, as bright and fresh as a springing sunbeam. But the crucible – the crucible was empty, drained, dry as a dried-out well, as a frosty stone, clean as a plate that a dog has fed from.

The mouse looked up. 'It has taken it all,' he said.

The alchemist nodded and smiled. 'Why, so it has!'

'It was the juice from the tongues of those flowers that did it,' the mouse cried, 'those curious spotted flowers – what was their name?'

The alchemist rubbed his chin. 'For the moment,' he said, 'I hardly remember. But I'll remember some day, I expect. And that may not be the only way. There may be other, better ways. Anyhow, I've been thinking – there's enough gold in this house for the time being.'

The mouse nodded slowly, because he understood.

'Go home now,' said the alchemist, 'it will soon be morning.'

'And – shall I come back tonight?'

'If you're interested in joining me.'

So the mouse went off to his mouse-hole, with a proud tilt to his golden whisker.

Next day the miller called in at the alchemist's house for a potion. He had an angry thumb, swollen as big as a bap, poisoned from a fish-hook that had lodged in it, for whenever the sails of his mill were idle he was out along the river with his rod.

'And I suppose you're still at the old game yourself,' he said to the alchemist.

The alchemist said he was.

'And where's your gold, eh? I've more to show from my fishing, when all's said and done. Well, nobody can say you ever put yourself out of a job. Tell me this, though, did you ever come near to it at all?'

'I did,' said the alchemist.

'Well, well. How near?'

The alchemist smiled. 'As near,' he said, 'as the breadth of a mouse's whisker.'

'Ah!' said the miller, and he nodded – nodded with sympathetic appreciation, because he was a fisherman himself.

Mary Patton
Of Mary F. Patton we know very little. In the 1924 edition of Maud
Joynt's *Golden Legends of the Gael* there is an elaborate frontispiece signed
by her. The story of Eonín comes from her collected *Turf Fire Tales* which
were published in 1935. All the creatures in Mary Patton's stories have a
distinct personality – her mermaids are like fussy maiden aunts and the
conger eel and Great Grey Seal converse like politicians.
Eonín was translated into Irish by Pádraic Óg Ó Conaire – an Irish
teacher, novelist, and member of the Dáil translation staff who was
overshadowed by his better-known namesake.

Eonín

Mary Patton

EONÍN WAS A LITTLE BOY who lived in Aran on the Big Island.
His home was a little out of Kilronan on the shore facing the
Galway coast, and was quite a comfortable one, for Eonín's
father owned a hooker and was well known and well
thought of in the three islands. Eonín was not old enough to
go to the fishing with his father as yet, for he had only just
begun to go to school, but he loved the sea and was never so
happy as when it was fine and his father would take him out
in the boat if he was only going out for a short time.

Sorcha, his mother, did not love the sea, and would never
set foot in the hooker, but stayed at home minding Una, the
baby, and keeping the house ready for Seán, her husband,
when he came in tired and wet after a night's fishing. She
dreaded the storms that blew in from the Atlantic so
suddenly, and would sit up half the night if Seán was out on
the water.

''Tis no use to be taking on so, woman dear,' said the old
grandmother, who sat in the warm corner by the fire. 'We
all must get death some time, and we may be taken on land
as well as on sea. We are all just in God's hands.'

'It is as God wills it indeed,' said Sorcha, only in her heart
she cried, 'Let him be spared to me this long while, Mother
of God!' And she looked at Eonín and wondered how she
would bring up the boy without the man to help her.

They were talking like this one evening, waiting for Seán

to come home, while Eonín was learning his lesson for the morrow by the fireside, and he began to wonder if he would hear his father coming up the road and giving a shout to let them know he was there, or would they carry him up in a sail like Seamus Rua. He was so relieved when he heard the usual call that he threw down his book and ran out of the house to meet him. It was bright moonlight and there was very little wind to make a noise at sea, but when Eonín was lifted up to his father's shoulder above the level of the loose stone wall he was sure he heard something besides the rattle of the pebbles as they were drawn back by the receding waves. It sounded like someone singing far out in the bay, and as Eonín was very fond of singing he sat quite still and listened till he was carried into the house and set down.

'There is music out on the sea,' he called out to his mother. 'Will you not come out and listen to it? It is lovely.'

'God stand between us and harm!' cried his mother, and she ran to the door and shut it tight to keep out the sound, for every Aran woman knows that if her son hears the mermaids singing he will be drowned in the end.

'The boats are coming in, and it is some of the men singing that he hears,' said Seán, laughing at her. 'You think too much of those sayings, Sorcha. We are learning better than that nowadays.' And he took Una out of her cradle to have a look at her, and danced her up and down till she screamed with delight.

'It is what I am always telling her,' said the grandmother from her corner; 'but indeed you are a good head to the house, Seán, and have never grudged me the best of tea and sugar or the bit of tobacco.' And she lit her pipe and smoked by the fire while Sorcha set the food out on the table.

It was early in the autumn when Sorcha came back from Kilronan saying that the old Protestant clergyman living in the Rectory there was ill and not likely to recover. He lived all alone, for his wife was dead and his daughter married abroad, and though he had very few of his own congregation he was well known and well liked by all the islanders, for he never interfered with anybody and gave a good price for the fish. So Sorcha was really sorry when she heard the news.

'And the housekeeper tells me,' she said, 'that she doesn't

49

know what she will do at all. The steamer will not be back for more than a week, and she has no way of sending to Galway to let them know. If the poor gentleman dies there will be no one to bury him.'

'There is a clergyman at Inverin on the mainland,' said Seán. 'I will go over and fetch him back,' and he glanced up at the sky as he spoke. Sorcha glanced too, for she knew the weather signs as well as he did, if not better. There was not much wind, but the clouds were very high and spread in narrow streamers, and there was a noise in the air that meant the sea was coming in a heavy swell through the sound.

'There will be no boats from Aran putting out for the fishing to-night,' she said.

'Think if it was myself lying there with no one of my own near me,' said Seán. 'It is but nine miles to Cashla; I will be back before the storm breaks.'

So he went down to the quay and hoisted sail for the mainland, while Sorcha went back into the house after she watched the hooker out of sight on the first long tack eastward.

The gale sprang up sooner than she expected, a real Aran squall, short in duration perhaps but violent enough while it lasted. Eonín coming back from school was nearly blown off his legs as he met the wind coming over the hill. He was astonished not to see his father when he got home.

'Is he gone out in the hooker?' he asked his mother.

'He is so!' she said. 'God send him home safe to us!'

She would say no more, but got Eonín his dinner and then sat down with some sewing for Una, to keep herself from thinking. It was too wild to go out, and Eonín tried to start a game of his own in a corner, but it was the longest evening he had ever known. His mother sewed silently, his granny sat talking to herself by the fire, and Una asleep in her cradle was the only comfortable one of the lot. He was not one bit sorry when his mother put down her work and said it was time for him to go to bed.

His bed was in a little room just off the living-room, and he could not tell how long he might have slept when he was wakened by a sound in the kitchen, and sitting up in bed he saw there was a light still there. He slipped from out the bed-clothes noiselessly, and creeping to the door opened it cautiously and peeped through. The turf fire was burning brightly and beside it his grandmother was still sitting. On the table was spread his father's usual supper, and in the window was a lighted candle and his mother sitting beside it with a look on her face he had never seen before.

'A great many of the Costellos got their death on the sea,' said the grandmother. 'My own man always said to me, "And isn't it better than lying on a bed ailing for weeks and all the money going out of the house to the doctor?"' But his mother made no answer except to burst into a fit of weeping. Then Eonín crept back and sat on the edge of his bed thinking a moment, for he knew that now as the only man in the house it was for him to be up and doing something.

Presently he reached for his clothes in the dark and pulled them on.

Seán's house was better built and more comfortable than most of the fishermen's houses in Aran, and the window in Eonín's bedroom could really open and shut. The wind was not on that side of the house, and moving carefully he slid up the lower sash and climbed out without the women hearing him. He closed the window behind him and stood in the little cabbage-plot.

The wind had commenced to slacken somewhat, and stars shone out here and there through the racing clouds. It was light enough to see his way to the stone wall which bounded the garden, and once over that he stood in the lane which reached to the shore. His skin shoes made no noise on the stones and no one knew that he had left the house or made any attempt to stop him as he ran towards a line of rocks which stretched out black among the surging waves.

Every Aran boy knows about mermaids, and some of them will tell you they have seen them. Eonín had never seen a mermaid, but he was a very little boy and his idea now was to scramble out to the farthest point of the rocks and see if he could find one. If he caught hold of her and held her tight she would have to tell him where his father was and promise to bring him home safe. So he slid and groped his way over the wet stones and slippery seaweed till he reached the farthest rock.

51

There was no mermaid to be seen looking up out of the water as he had half expected, and he did not know if they would hear him if he called out to them. He knelt down on the rock and tried to look through the heavy mass of weed. As he did so a huge wave swept over the rock entirely submerging it, and carrying Eonín fighting and struggling for breath back with it into the very depths of the sea.

How far he was falling he could not tell, but after the first horrible choking sensation was over he seemed to be sinking quite easily through the water till he came with a bump on something that heaved and writhed and twisted around him with a queer hissing sound. Eonín rolled off it and found himself lying on a broad ledge of rock with a huge conger eel coiled on it staring at him.

'Now who have I here?' said the conger, when he had recovered a little from the shock.

'God and Mary save you,' said Eonín, 'and it's little manners you have not to give me the greeting.'

'Where would I get manners,' said the conger, 'living in this backward place? The People of the Sea do not care much for my society, and if it were not for the Fox Sharks and the Sword-fish I would have no one to associate with. But who are you, and where do you come from?'

'I am Eonín, the son of big Seán Costello,' said Eonín, 'and I live on the Strand road a little way from Kilronan.'

'I know big Seán the fisherman,' said the conger. 'Indeed he is well known in all the seas of Aran. When I was a little fellow only a foot and a half long he caught me in his net and threw me back into the water. 'Grow a bit more,' he said 'before I catch you again.' A meaner man would have used me for bait. I have always had a great wish for Seán ever since then and I am pleased to see his son, and you may tell him that I am ten feet long, and can bite through a man's hand. I am not like the little yellow congers of the sand. I think he would be a proud man if he could catch me now.'

'I may never tell my father anything about you,' Eonín sobbed. 'He has never reached home to-night, and it was trying to find where he is that I came to be here.'

'Tell me all about it,' said the conger, coiling himself up again to listen.

So Eonín told him how he had gone out to find a

mermaid, and how a big wave had swept the rock and sucked him under.

'I have no great opinion of the mermaids,' said the conger when Eonín had told him the whole story. 'They are too interfering and too fond of coming between an honest fish and his food. Telling the hake where I am lying indeed! A conger has to get on in the world as well as another. I would be living on jellyfish if they had their own way.

'I can show you where the mermaids live, but more than that I cannot promise, for the truth is we are not friends at all. They think too much of themselves with their songs and their golden combs for their hair. It's very little cause they have for pride to my mind,' he went on. 'Have they tails like mine or teeth like mine? Is there one of them could crunch a lobster as I can? However, since you want to see them I will take you down, for they live lower down than I do, and I would be glad to do a service to the son of big Seán the fisherman.'

So he flattened the great fin that ran from his head to his tail and told Eonín to put his arms around his neck and stretch himself along his back, and when he was settled firmly the conger shot head first off the rock and dived downwards with a beautiful swift motion.

They landed at last on a bed of the most beautiful white sand Eonín had ever seen. There were beautiful seaweeds of various colours growing here and there, and all kinds of shining shells. Around the sands great rocks towered up, and in the rocks were caves from one of which came a sound of very sweet singing.

'If you go straight in there,' said the conger, pointing with his side fin at this cave, 'you will find them at their antics. And put a bold face on you, and ask for what you want, and do not give in to them, or let them put upon you. I am sorry I cannot go in with you, but I would not give them the satisfaction of finding me here. So now good-bye, and I wish you luck.'

He shot off up through the water, and Eonín was left alone. He felt a little scared, especially after what the conger had said about the mermaids, but the singing inside the cave was so sweet it drew him towards it, and at last he took courage to enter.

53

He found himself in a great hall formed out of the rock. It was not dark as he had thought a cave would be, but lit with the pale green light that seemed to represent daylight under the water. The floor was of shining sand and the roof seemed made of masses of floating seaweed through which the fish came darting.

But Eonín could look at nothing but the mermaids. There were a great many of them, and some of them were floating and swimming about pretending to chase the fish, while the rest were gathered in a group singing the song that had attracted him in. They stopped as he stood at the entrance, and turned and looked at him, and he thought they could not be as unkind as the conger had made out, for they had very sweet faces though their long hair was of a strange greenish golden colour and they had long tails like a fish, covered with silver scales. They gathered round Eonín, smiling and holding out their hands, and then he saw that there was one who seemed taller than the others seated on a rock at the end of the hall. She was leaning her head on her hand as if thinking, and when she raised it he saw she was more beautiful and that she wore a band of shining stones around her head. She looked up and beckoned with her hand.

'You are very welcome, Eonín, son of big Seán the fisherman,' said the mermaid of the rock. 'Now, what have you come seeking?'

'The big conger said that my father might be with you,' said Eonín, when he had recovered from his astonishment at finding they knew who he was. 'But I do not think you would harm him,' he added.

'I will take you to see him,' said the mermaid, 'but you must tell me first, are you a brave boy?'

'I am a very brave boy,' said Eonín. 'I go down through the Fairies' Gap to the well in the dusk of the evening if my mother wants water for the house, and there are bigger boys than I am in Aran who will not do that.'

'That is well,' said the mermaid; 'and now you may come with me.'

She took him in her arms and swam swiftly with him across the cave and out into the space beyond till they came to another ridge of rocks thickly covered with brown weed. She set Eonín on the top of this and told him to look over. There was another stretch of sand at the foot of the ridge, and there Eonín saw his father lying as if asleep. His head was resting on one arm and his body rocked slightly with the motion of the water.

'Can I not go and wake him?' asked Eonín. 'He would be terribly vexed to be lying there asleep and my mother wanting him at home.'

'No,' said the mermaid, 'you may not wake him.'

'Will you not let him go back, and we all of us wanting him so bad? My mother will lose her life if you will not let him go.'

'There is a rule of life under the sea as well as on the land,' said the mermaid, 'and I may not let him go for the asking. But if you will stay with us and take his place, we may let him go back.'

55

A terrible dread came over Eonín at the thought of staying down at the bottom of the sea and never going home to his mother and Una again, and all he could say for the moment was, 'Is that the way it is?' 'That is the way, and no other way,' said the mermaid.

'Then I will stay,' said Eonín with a great sob, 'for I am not big enough to take out the hooker, and there will be no head to the house if my father does not go home. But I will be terribly lonesome away from them all.' The tears came into his eyes and he would have burst out crying only he remembered he had said he was brave.

'See,' said the mermaid, 'your father is no longer there.' And when he looked there was nothing but the sand to be seen. Then she placed her hand over his heart and it was so cold that he felt the chill right through his body, and she kissed him on the forehead till his life on land faded out of his mind, and he forgot his home and his people and was as gay and happy as if he had never thought of missing them.

The days passed by, though you could only tell night from day by the green light becoming darker and lighter. There was no sun or moon or stars to be seen, and indeed Eonín had forgotten all about them. Soon he could swim and float quite well, but if the mermaids wished to take him any distance they put him astride a huge codfish so that he might keep up with them easily. He soon found that they were not always playing or singing but had quite a lot to do, tidying up the rock-pools after a storm, looking after the fishes and seeing that the smaller ones were not oppressed by the bigger.

When the mermaids went to tidy the rock-pools they always took Eonín with them, and he would help them to clear away the torn seaweed and see that the anemones and sea-urchins were fast on their rocks, and play with the little red rock-fish. But sometimes they had something to do of

which they never spoke to him.

He was never left quite alone until the day after a great storm had been raging overhead for many hours. He thought they would have had a great expedition round the pools seeing what damage had been done, but instead they told him he must play by himself for a while, as they must all go away and could not take him where they were going.

He did as he was told and tried to amuse himself playing with the shells that lay about the sand, but it was dull work all alone, and presently he strayed out of the cave on to the stretch of sand outside. Something dark shot through the water overhead, and presently the big conger landed beside him. Eonín had no recollection of anything that had happened before the mermaid kissed him, so he only looked at the conger wondering who he was and what had brought him.

'Well, and how do you get on with them?' said the conger, who as we know had no manners.

Eonín only looked at him in a puzzled way. 'Do you mean the mermaids?' he said. 'They are all away somewhere.'

'There is a big wreck off the Hag's Head,' said the conger, 'and they have all gone off to look after the drowned sailors. I have not often a good word for them, but I like to be just, and I will say this, they show every respect and care for the drowned. It is only when you are alive that they torment you. But are you content to be here, and do you never think of going back to your home?'

'What is home?' asked Eonín. 'I live here, and I play with the fishes and the shells and I help the mermaids to settle the pools after a storm. I do not know of any other kind of life.'

'I see they have been playing their tricks with you,' said the conger, 'but I know a cure for that, and I will fetch it straight away, for indeed I have come to talk to you on a matter of some importance. Now do not stir from this till I come back.'

And he shot up through the water, leaving the boy staring after him. He was gone some little time, and Eonín wondered if he was really coming back.

By and by he saw the conger shooting swiftly downwards. He carried something in his mouth.

'Take this bit of seaweed out of my mouth and eat it,' he told Eonín.

It was reddish-brown with notched edges and had a salt taste. As Eonín chewed it he suddenly knew it was 'Dulsk' or dry seaweed he was eating, and the memory of the life he used to lead on land came back to him. He could see his home standing back a little from the road, and the fields covered with grey slabs of stone, and the little white cabins of Kilronan in the distance. He remembered his mother and father and little sister, and his granny who sat always in her corner near the fire, the hooker lying beside the quay and the sunlight shining on the water. An immense grief and a longing to be back again came over him.

'Do you remember where you came from?' asked the conger, eyeing him curiously. But Eonín could not speak, his heart was so full.

'It is what I came to talk to you about,' said the conger, 'for there is no peace or rest for the dwellers among the rocks of Aran. Day and night men are searching with poles and grappling-irons till the congers are driven from their homes and dare not return. And so it came into my mind that it is you they are seeking, and you must go back if we are to have any life at all.'

'How will I go back?' said Eonín. 'Now that I remember, I have a terrible wish to go home.'

'I will carry you on my back,' said the conger, 'and leave you on the very rock you fell in off, if you will put your arms round my neck and hold on tight.'

But a sudden fear came over Eonín. 'I said I would stay here instead of my father,' he cried, 'and so I cannot go. He would come back himself if he knew I had gone back on my word, and my mother could not do without him. So I must stay with the mermaids.'

He cried bitterly, for the more he remembered the harder it was not to go.

'You have very inconvenient notions,' said the conger. 'And if this is your decision, the congers may leave Aran, for there will be no end to this searching. When they call out to your father that it is useless to go on, and to give up, he cries out he will search all his life. There is but one thing now that I can think of doing, and I do not think it can be any harm.

We must go out to Skerdmore and consult the Great Grey Seal who lives there. He says he is a cousin of the mermaids and is sometimes taken for them. He may be able to tell us some way of getting over the difficulty.'

Then the conger flattened the fin on his back and Eonín lay along it and put his arms round the conger's neck and away they shot through the water. They went very fast, but it was a long way to Skerdmore, and Eonín's arms began to ache from holding on so tightly, when they rose suddenly to the surface of the sea. Then he saw they had reached a tiny island with a great many rocks showing on one side of it, and on one of these was lying a great grey seal.

The conger hooked his tail round a point of the rock, and Eonín scrambled up on to it.

'We have come to consult your Honour on a difficult point,' said the conger very politely, for he knew the Grey Seal could have bitten him in two, 'and we hope that you will give us the benefit of your great wisdom and learning. Here is a little boy who has been living with the mermaids in order to release his father, and now he would like to go home himself if he could do so without breaking his promise.'

'The mermaids are distant relations of mine,' said the Grey Seal, raising himself on his two front flippers. 'We are both musical and you may have heard me singing. I should not care to annoy them at the request of a mere conger. Why should this little boy want to go home?'

'It is because I have remembered my home and my mother and my father,' said Eonín, 'and all the things I used to do on land. My mother will have no one to get in the water for the house, or to be running in when my father is away at the fishing. But I would not vex the mermaids or go unless they would let me.'

'We all know,' said the conger, 'that there are a great deal too many boys in this world, and that they are good for very little except to throw stones at the seals and disturb them by splashing round the rocks, but there is more at stake in this matter than you might think. The fate of all the congers of Aran depends on his going home. We have no rest or peace while they are searching for him, and if we are driven away we shall no longer be able to listen to the lovely music

59

which you make on the summer nights.'

'I see, I see,' said the Grey Seal, greatly pleased. 'Since you like my voice I should be sorry if you had no opportunity of hearing it. But it will not be easy for him to win his release. There is a rule of life under the sea as well as on land, and they may not let him go for the asking.'

'What am I to do?' asked Eonín.

'You will have to find out what they want most in the world,' said the Grey Seal, 'and then you will have to give it to them.'

Eonín's heart sank, for he could not think how he could accomplish such a task, but the conger thanked the seal profusely and asked Eonín to get on his back again.

'I am always pleased to help anyone who appreciates music,' said the Grey Seal.

They left the seal on his rock bellowing most dismally and made all speed back to the mermaids' cave. The night had fallen and with all their haste the mermaids were there before them, so that when they reached the entrance they heard them singing softly inside.

'Now go in,' said the conger, 'and keep your wits about you and do not fail me, for it would break my heart to live even as far off as Inishbofin. I will wait behind the rocks here to see what happens.'

Eonín slowly went in, wondering what he should say and how he would get them what they wanted most in the world even if he could find it out. They were all seated round the cave and none of them playing, but singing so sad an air that it brought the tears to his eyes. The mermaid who always sat at the end on the rock beckoned to him, and when he reached her she lifted him up on to her lap.

'Now, Eonín,' she said, 'tell me all that is in your heart.'

Eonín laid his head against her breast and told her all that had happened since they left him alone.

'I have a sore longing to get home,' he said, when he had finished his story, 'and so will you please tell me what you want most in the world and I will try and get it for you.'

The mermaid looked very thoughtful and then she signed to the others, who all stopped singing and gathered round her.

'Now I will tell you, Eonín,' she said, 'when there is a

wreck on the coast we go to look after those that may be drowned, and we sing to them that they may rest peacefully until they are called from our care. We know a great many songs, both gay and sad, but to-night we need one that we have never heard or learned. Can you sing us a song that we do not know?'

Then Eonín thought of all the songs he had ever heard and he sang them the songs the fishermen sing when the boats are coming in, or when they are raising the nets or hauling at the ropes, but the mermaids shook their heads and looked sorrowful and said they knew all those.

'It will be some English song you are wanting,' he cried, 'and I have no English.'

'No, no,' they cried, 'it is not that we want at all.'

Then Eonín suddenly bethought him of a song they could never have heard, for when his mother sang it she shut the door tight to keep out the sound of the sea. She sang it always to put Una to sleep and he knew it well. He lifted up his voice and sang, 'Oh, little head of gold. Oh, candle of the house –' and they listened without a word till he came to the very end.

'That is the song we want!' they all cried when he had finished, 'and now we will show you why we want it.'

They swam with him to another part of the cave, and there, lying asleep on a bed made of the softest sea-moss, he saw a tiny child, not much bigger than Una and with golden curls shining against the dark green weed.

'We knew no song that she would have cared to hear,' they said; 'but now you have taught us one. You have earned your release, though we are sorry to lose you.'

The tallest mermaid lifted him on to her lap again and she placed her hand on his heart and kissed him on the lips, but this time her lips and her hands were so warm that he felt the warmth right through his body, and when she had done that she looked him in the eyes and smiling said: 'Now all that has happened shall be as though it has never happened, and the conger shall take you to the very rock you fell in off.'

They called the conger in, and when he knew that he was to take him home his delight knew no bounds, and he span round and round to show how pleased he was till they all

61

felt quite giddy and told him he should not have as much as a sprat to eat if he did not stop. Then he calmed down, and they placed Eonín on his back when they had all said good-bye, and stood waving their hands and singing while he shot up out of sight with his burden.

'I too will say good-bye,' said the conger when Eonín had scrambled off his back on to the rock. 'I must now go and tell the other congers the great news that you are back ánd that there will be no more searching of the rocks. And mind you tell your father I am ten feet long and can bite through a man's hand. I think he will be proud to hear of me again.'

'We will go fishing for you together,' cried Eonín, and the conger waved his side fin and sank down through the water.

Eonín found himself alone lying on the rock, and as he looked round and saw the familiar scene his life under the sea faded out of his mind and he could not quite tell why he was on the rock or what had brought him there. The sun had risen and the storm had passed over. The sky was quite clear and the sun shining, and except that the sea was still rather rough there was no trace of a gale. He stood up and saw a hooker running into the harbour and knew it for his father's boat. By running quickly he reached the quay as it came alongside, and in it was his father safe and sound and another man in the stern wrapped in a dark overcoat.

'What brings you out here at this hour, Eonín?' said his father, for it was still very early. 'But since you are here, run home with á message from me, for I must show this gentleman the way to the Rectory. Tell your mother we could not get out of Cashla the way the wind was, and that that was the delay, for I am sure she was uneasy.'

Eonín ran back hard and met his mother on the pathway, for she too had seen the hooker.

'How did you get out without my seeing you?' she asked, bewildered, when he had given the message; but she was too happy to scold, and he ran on in, not quite sure of how it had happened himself.

Sometimes when he is making up a story for Una it all comes back to him, and he tells it to her, while she listens with great attention, sucking her thumb the while. But he can get no one else to believe him when he says he has talked with the Great Grey Seal at Skerdmore.

Pádraig Ó Siochfhradha (1883-1964) – ('An Seabhac')
All really great literatures have produced at least one famous antagonist
or scapegoat. American children enjoy the adventures of Huckleberry
Finn and English children, of course, can still read about William. Both
characters have that special combination of mischievousness and naiveté
which appeals to the daredevil in every small child who finds himself
getting into scrapes.
We have had to go to the well-known Irish language author 'An
Seabhac' for our 'William'. 'An Seabhac' (The Hawk) is the pseudonym
of Pádraig Ó Siochfhradha whose book *Jimín Mháire Thaidhg* was first
published in 1921. For many years Irish-speaking children have been
able to enjoy the adventures of the intrepid Jimeen – now, thanks to the
first translation by Patricia Egan, Peter Fallon and Íde ní Laoghaire,
English-speaking children can share in the fun. Through all his
adventures and escapades Jimeen is, at the end of the day, usually more
sinned against than sinner.

Christmas
Pádraig Ó Siochfhradha

An excerpt, translated from the Irish of
Jimín Mháire Thaidhg

I MUST TELL YOU about the Christmas we had. Mam went to
Dingle a few days before it – herself and Dad – and they took
the horse and cart, with a creel and box in the cart.

Mam had the money and she took two geese with her –
one for the vet and one for the bank manager, because he's
the man who minds her money and she thinks the world of
him.

While they were in Dingle, I went off to Glenadown with
the big knife and some string and brought home a big holly
bush, and I got some ivy in the ruins of the church.

As I was passing her door, Nell-Mary-Andy came out and
was buttering me up trying to get me to give her some holly.
She thought she'd make a right little eejit of me, praising me
and calling me a 'good little boy', and promising me a
Christmas present! I pretended, at first, that I wouldn't give

her any. But, when I untied the bundle at home, I took a couple of branches over. I'm very great with Nell, you know.

Cait was all excited when she saw the big load I was bringing in.

'Oh!' said she, 'we'll make the house lovely,' and she was looking at the red berries on the holly and dancing around the floor. 'Oh, aren't they beautiful?' said she. 'Did you ever see such a lovely red?'

That's the way Cait always goes on, even if it's only a daisy or a bunch of cowslips. All the girls are like that, about all kinds of things.

I was hungry.

'Stop your messing,' said I, 'is there anything to eat?'

'Oh! I forgot,' said Cait and she began to whisper. 'You won't tell what I've made, will you?'

'What?' said I.

She laughed.

'I won't tell you, because you'd tell Mam.'

'I swear I won't,' said I.

'She'll kill me over the sugar,' said Cait.

'What sugar?' said I.

'And because of the cream!' said she.

'Crikey, Cait, have you made sweet cakes!'

'Oh, I won't tell you, I won't tell you,' said she, laughing and jumping up and down. Then she went to the dresser and took down two cups.

'Ah! Cait,' said I, 'tell me what you have.'

'I won't, I won't,' said she, and she laughed, dancing and kicking up her heels. She didn't see the ivy on the floor until it tripped her up and, lo and behold, didn't she break a big piece off the rim of one of the cups.

Cait picked it up and she was trembling as she tried to fix it back in place. She started to cry, and then didn't she try to put the blame on me! I soon told her that it was herself and her jumping around. But there was no point in talking. All she'd do was cry.

I ended up feeling sorry for her.

'Give it to me, Cait,' said I, 'and Mam won't ever know about it.'

I took the cup to the dresser and put it under two other

cups with the broken side facing in.

'What will I do if Mam finds it?' said Cait.

Then we each had a mug of tea. That was when Cait brought out the things she'd made – little cream cakes with sugar icing on them. We got butter in the cupboard and I spotted a big pot of jam with the top tied tight. I cut the knot easily and we enjoyed all the things we had. We put a full spoon of jam on every bit of bread.

When we'd eaten our fill, the jam was well down in the pot, but I tied the paper on again and put it back in the cupboard where it had been. It's a pity Mam doesn't go to Dingle every day!

Then I got a hammer and little nails and Cait handed me the holly and ivy. We nailed it around the window, and on top of the dresser, and over the fireplace. It was hard to fix it where there was no wood, and I had to drive big nails into the wall. From time to time huge chunks of mortar fell.

When we'd finished the house, we grabbed Sailor – that's the dog – and covered him from head to tail with holly, and had a great laugh at him. When evening came we lit the lamp. The house looked lovely.

It was dark when Mam and Dad came home. We thought Mam'd be delighted but, to tell the truth, she caused ructions when she saw the lumps of mortar missing from the walls. I had to disappear until she calmed down. It's hard to please some people!

The following day Cait told me what Mam brought from Dingle: nine big long candles standing in the creel, three of them red. They were as tall as the window, and she brought a box full of raisins, and one of sugar, and of tea, as well as a big barm brack from the shop. There were bottles too – some with yellow drink in them and others with something purple, and a big jug full of black stuff. She had a big lump of meat too. I heard she brought apples, too, but I didn't even get one that night because of the damage we'd done with the nails. She put everything into the cupboard and locked it.

Next day Mam killed a goose and a duck. When the goose was cold, she put paper round its head and plucked it and left it hanging on the back of the door.

We had a great time on Christmas Eve. Cait and myself

got two big turnips and cut them in half and made a hole in each of them to stand the candles in. Then we stuck little branches of holly in them and Cait put a frill of paper around them. They were lovely and we lit them long before it was dark; but Mam put them out again.

That night, Mam put potatoes and fish on the table for us but neither myself nor Cait ate a single bit, because we knew other things were on the way. After a while, Mam took out the big brack and cut it for us. Then she made tea, and gave us an apple each.

When Mickileen's father passed by the door, Mam called him in and gave him a drop from a bottle with three stars on it. She gave Dad a drop too. Then she got a drink for herself from another bottle and then they all said, 'May we all be alive this time next year', whatever they meant by that.

Big-Betty and Mary-Andy came in next and Mam put a drop from the yellow bottle into two glasses, added sugar and boiling water, and stirred them with a spoon. At first I thought they wouldn't touch it. Mary-Andy said, 'Oh! A drop of that would kill me!' But she downed it all the same, and it didn't kill her either!

As the night wore on, a lot of young men came in and Mam gave them their drinks out of the big jug.

When I saw them all drinking, I got an unmerciful longing for a drink, myself.

When Dad went out with Mickileen's father and Mam was talking to the women over by the fire, I took a swig out of the jug. It's a wonder the taste didn't kill me. I couldn't swallow it back, and was afraid to spit it out on the floor. I ran out the door with my mouth full. Mam saw me.

'Where are you off to, now, Jimeen?' said she, but I couldn't say a word. I opened the door and spat. She followed, and saw me coughing and wiping my mouth.

'Ha-ha,' said she, 'I wouldn't put it past you, you rascal. Weren't you the nosey one?'

It was horrible stuff.

It was late when we went to bed that night, because Mam was getting the goose ready for Christmas Day. She cleaned it out and washed it, and then stuffed it with boiled potatoes and onions and salt and pepper and butter and loads of other things. She sewed it up with thread. Myself and Cait

were watching her.

On Christmas morning Cait and Mam went to first Mass. Myself and Dad were left in charge. When Dad was milking the cows, I went to look at the things in the cupboard. I took an apple and filled my pockets with raisins. There was a piece of brack cut, so I took that too.

When I was closing the cupboard, a thought struck me – I took the yellow bottle and half-filled a cup. I tasted it, but boy, as bad as the black stuff was the night before, the yellow drink was seven times worse. It would burn the throat off you. I didn't know what to do with it. I called the dog and put the cup under his nose but he wouldn't look at it. All he did was sneeze.

Then I thought of another plan. I got a fistful of meal, wet it with the stuff from the bottle, and left it on a plate in the yard. The big gander gulped it all down. At first I didn't notice anything odd about him. Then he began to cackle. He stopped after a while, and started walking around with his head to one side. Round and round he went in a circle. Then he stopped, spread his legs apart and started shaking himself backwards and forwards. He'd make the cats laugh. Then he lay down and closed his eyes, for all the world like Old-Dermot when he dozes in the big chair by the fire.

Finally, he lay flat out on the ground, stretched his neck, spread his wings, and there wasn't a trace of life in him. It was as if he were dead. I was terrified that he'd die – and I didn't know what to do. I heard Dad coming in from the cowhouse and ran inside. When Dad saw the gander he stopped and started talking to himself.

'Upon my word, but that fellow's really plastered,' he said. 'Jimeen,' he yelled. I was sweeping the floor like mad. I came to the door.

'What did you do to the gander?' said Dad.

I stopped. I didn't like to hide the truth on Christmas morning, so I told Dad the story, in fits and starts. I could see he wasn't pleased.

'You'll pay for your tricks some day, my boy,' said he. 'And I suppose it was you finished off the cat, too, down in Poulalin?'

I thought I'd fall out of my standing. I didn't think a living soul knew about that. I felt sheepish then. I thought, of course, that Dad would tell Mam everything. I went to Mass and prayed all through it that God would keep me safe from all the trouble threatening me.

When I came home, Mam had the gander beside the fire, and he was recovering. She never found out what had happened to him because, when Dad came home, she was trying to find out from him who'd come in that morning and got whiskey.

Dad was making a joke of the whole thing and wouldn't tell her. He threw me a look that left me feeling quite uneasy.

Still, Dad's all right.

Bad Blood
Eilís Dillon

IN THE EARLY, EARLY MORNING the lake was utterly still, John could see it from his bedroom window, laid out smoothly like a sheet of white satin, reflecting the white sky. Here and there, just above the surface, little puffs of mist floated. Each one certainly contained the spirit of a magician, just disappeared after his night's work. The lake was not wide here, so that he could see the tall thin reeds at the far side, motionless, doubling their length in the water below. The coots and water-hens were still asleep, or at least they had not yet come out to splash and paddle and scurry up and down at the edge of the reed-beds.

For the hundredth time, John wished he had a boat. With his father's land running down to the edge of the lake, it was never possible to forget the delights that he must miss. On such a morning as this, he would slide his boat into the water softly, so as not to disturb it with the smallest ripple. He could almost feel the boat grinding on the shingle, crushing with a dry crackling sound the hollow pieces of reed that lay everywhere along the shore, then floating erect and free. The keel would touch bottom for a moment at the bows as he stepped in, and then rise a little out of the water as he moved to the stern. A long gentle push with one oar would turn the bows out towards the middle of the lake. Then he would settle on the thwart and slide both oars into the stirrup-shaped rowlocks and move off, dipping as softly as a fishing swan, sending a great right-angular line washing away towards the shore.

But he had no boat. Mike Boyle, their neighbour in the next farm, owned a boat, but John must never borrow it. There was bad blood between John's family and the Boyles, and John must always be very careful not to make matters worse. But they were already as bad as they could be, he thought, because the bad blood was directly reponsible for the fact that John had no boat. There had been a lawsuit

71

about boundaries and drainage, and it had cost so much that there could be no talk of boats until the lawyers had been paid. 'Next year, perhaps,' his father had said. Next year might come, John thought, but 'next year perhaps' was a long way off.

A fish pushed his nose half an inch above the calm surface of the lake, sending a widening circle travelling slowly in every direction. Just as the centre of the circle became still, the fish jumped again, as if he had enjoyed the effect of what he had done the first time. John took a line from the drawer of his cupboard and examined it to see that it had a hook on the end. It was a home-made line. He had no fishing-rod, but the line would have been all right from a boat. On his quiet way out of the house he passed through the kitchen and collected the little wad of sour dough that he kept handy at all times. It was not that he meant to fish, but it just didn't seem right to go down to the lake without a line.

Everything was white this morning, even the dew on the grass, lying heavy in white beads, in a way that it never did after rain. He took off his sandals and brushed through the grass, expertly avoiding the occasional short, strong thistles. In a few hours this field would be a torment of horseflies, but now it was too early for them. Over by the single elm tree, the cattle were all clustered together, still lying half asleep in the wet grass. They were Kerry cows, great milkers, never complaining, and providing an endless supply of silky, big-eared calves as black as themselves, and with short, trembling tails. Some of the cows turned slow, friendly heads to look at him as he passed, but they did not get up.

The field ended at the edge of the lake, sloping steeply for the last few yards. The grass was cropped short here, for it was the favourite grazing ground of the cattle since the warm weather had begun. They liked to step into the lake and cool their feet, in the hot part of the day.

The boundary hedge between the two farms began to thin as it neared the shingle. Where the hedge finished there was only a single wire, stretching from the last thorn bush to a stake planted out in the lake. It was a flimsy arrangement, but it served well enough.

The short pieces of dried reed tickled the soles of his feet.

He hopped like a bird over the shingle, with bent knees and eyes down, watching for sharp stones. When he was standing in the ice-cold water so that it bit at his toes, he looked up at last.

Then he saw the heifer. Immediately, it seemed as if his blood stopped flowing, as if he would never breathe nor move again. He knew the heifer. She was a Jersey, and she belonged to Mike Boyle. He had a little herd of these beautiful animals. Secretly and with shame, John loved those cows as he had never loved his own. Everything about them was perfect, their pale brown colouring, shading to cream underneath, their elegant, bony bodies, their slow intelligent faces and their gentle, confiding natures. John's greatest ambition was to own a herd of Jersey cattle, some wonderful day when he would have a farm of his own. He could see their richly yellow milk singing into big

galvanized buckets. No one would ever milk them except himself, no one. Often he had peered unseen through the boundary hedge and had seen Mike Boyle carelessly herding his cattle home without love or interest. From these secret watchings, John knew every one of them as well as their owner did.

He recognized the heifer at once, though there was so little of her to be seen. She was far out in the lake, so far that only her long back and her uplifted, frightened head showed above the water. There she stood, quite motionless. Only for the unnatural upward tilt of her neck, one would have thought that she was just enjoying a cooling bath. She was carrying her first calf, he knew. This was probably why she could not turn easily now and come ashore. He was quite certain that if no one came to her aid, she would stand there until she became exhausted and dropped into the water to drown. The thought make him a little sick.

He delayed no longer. A boat was necessary. If he had had a boat of his own he would have used it, but since he had not, he must use Boyle's boat. There it was, a strong, grey-painted one, lying drawn up just clear of the water line. He knew where the oars were, stuck in a leafy thorn bush right near the boat.

In a flash he had skipped under the wire, not feeling the sharp stones on the soles of his feet now. He brought out the oars one by one, burying his face deep among the sweet, shining leaves of the whitethorn. First one and then the other went into the boat. Then he sent it sliding down across the shingle, crushing the hollow reeds with a soft, dry, crackling sound. When the stern was well afloat he pushed off with a gentle oar so as not to frighten the heifer. He slid the oars into the rowlocks and began to row towards her.

She turned a huge, round, terrified eye on him when he came near.

'Silly little gom,' he said gently. 'Be quiet for just a minute more, just one minute.'

Edging the boat near to her, he patted her wet neck once. Then he took the long mooring-rope that lay coiled in the bows of the boat, made a slip knot in the end of it and quickly passed it over one of her horns.

'And now, oh God in heaven, please don't let her

stumble, for if she does she'll certainly drown. If Mike Boyle were to see me now, he might even think that I had led his heifer out into the lake to make an end of her.'

He glanced uneasily towards Boyle's house, but there was no sign of life there, no smoke from the chimney and no sheepdog nosing around. His own house was quiet too. It would be just as bad if his father were to come down to the edge of the lake and perhaps call out advice to him, frightening the heifer. John was determined that if he got that heifer ashore, he would never tell a soul about her adventure. He felt in his bones that as sure as he did, he would somehow be blamed for the whole affair.

He pulled gently on the rope. This had the effect of drawing the boat nearer to the heifer, so that her eyes widened still further. He let go of the rope at once. There was only one way to do it. He sat on the thwart, facing the bows of the boat, and took the oars in his hands. When he lifted them, the heifer jerked her head away in fright. He dropped the oars very slowly into the water and pulled once. First she just stretched her neck to follow the pull, and then she took one step.

'Come along, come along,' he said coaxingly. 'Patience and perseverance brought the snail to Jerusalem.'

She took another step. A splash of water washed against her nostrils, so that she spluttered. He waited in agony while she tossed her head once. If she were to bellow now, Mike Boyle might come running. It would soon be getting-up time. Cows like music, he remembered. He sang a little song for her in Irish. It was one that he had learned at school, about a red-backed cow with a single horn. The heifer seemed pleased, and she took another step, with her eyes fixed on him. Now she had turned, so that she was facing the shore. She must not be hurried. She must not be frightened. One downward plunge of her head and she might never come up again.

Two more steps and her flanks showed a little above the water. Still she held her head high, though there were six inches now between her chin and the surface of the lake. Slowly, slowly he drew her along. The boat moved heavily, because it was travelling the wrong way, but it was a well-balanced boat. The heifer did not lift her feet high, and thus she was able to feel and avoid the bigger stones that lay in her path.

John glanced over the side from moment to moment. The sun had come up, and spiralling lines of light glittered downwards through the water. They picked out the white stones shadowed with brown mud. Now the heifer was coming a little faster as the water became shallow. Before the stern of the boat could touch on the shingle, he slid the oars aboard and hopped out into the water. The boat rocked, and sent a wave splashing against her knees, but it did not matter now. He slipped the knot off her horn and led her, holding the same horn, right up on to the grass. He waited for a moment then, almost as if he had expected her to thank him for his services, but she just swished her sodden tail and lumbered off. All at once she seemed to become furiously hungry, for she began to tear up huge mouthfuls of grass as if she had been starved for a week.

John was deeply satisfied. It hardly seemed right that he should not be rewarded for his intelligence and efficiency. He swaggered down to the edge of the lake again and suddenly stooped for a stone and sent it spinning off across the flat water, leaving a dozen rings in its trail as if a line of fishes had all jumped together.

He had to wade knee-deep to the boat, which had sat still exactly where he had left it. The mooring-rope was soaked. If Mike Boyle were to see it before it had time to dry, he would know that the boat had been used. John picked the rope out of the water and began to turn the bows towards the shore. Then he stopped. Here, of course, was his reward. He would go fishing. Not for long, because he must be back with the boat before breakfast, but long enough to try for that bold fish that had jumped twice in two minutes.

Four strokes of the oars took himself and the boat out of sight of Boyle's house, so that he could pause and take out his line and bait it with the dough, and drop it overboard from the stern. He might get a pike. They would snap at anything. Trout have more delicate tastes. No one would want to eat a pike, but if it were a big one, its size would make up for that. He would show it to the family at once, and then keep it to show to the boys in the evening. The trouble would be to put it in a place where the cats wouldn't find it. That black cat Mulligan would nose out a fish half a mile away. Paddy the yardman swore that he had seen him fishing, but Paddy was a noted liar.

Hardly touching the water with the oars, John sent the boat sliding along, further and further away from home. The line trailed slackly. It should have had a fly on the end, he thought, if it were to catch a trout. Suddenly he realized that he did not care if he caught nothing, it was so pleasant just to float along under the white sky, watching the mist lift and flutter and blow away, and hearing the soft, dry, swinging song of the rushes all around him.

It was only by chance that his eye was on it when the line suddenly tightened. He let go of the oars and waited until there was a jerk. Within ten seconds he had plunged forward and flipped the fish into the boat. For a moment he was sorry for it as it panted for breath. Then when it lay still he was filled with a bursting triumph, that had to be let loose in a mighty yell. It was a trout, a huge one. It should only have liked flies, but it had accepted a bit of mouldy, sour dough and now it was his. He wished he could go sailing up and down that lake for ever, filling Mike Boyle's boat with mountains of monstrous fish until the water washed over the gunwale. But it was Mike's boat and it was time to return it.

He placed the trout carefully where he could see it. Then he turned the boat in a great swinging curve. The lake was so wide here that its further edge was only a blue-grey line. Another boat was coming towards him, a slow-moving black boat, probably from one of the remote villages up there by the lake-side. The people from those villages were as slow and as black as their boats. They wore black clothes and black hats, and they would scarcely look at you to pass the time of day as they rowed down towards the town. John had found them unfriendly and silent too, when he had gone with his father in a hired boat to buy a sheep from them. Now he measured the distance between himself and the other boat, and he was glad to see that he would have turned in towards the shore before the other would have come abreast of him. Thus occupied, he never once glanced behind him until he was almost ashore on the beach below Mike Boyle's house. And there, standing at the water's edge, so close that the toes of his huge boots were awash, was Mike Boyle himself.

Though his legs were short, his body seemed to have been made for a taller man, thick and strong and heavy about the neck and shoulders. His habit of leaning forward on the balls of his feet gave him a threatening appearance, as if he were always prepared to strike out with his ready fists. His eyes were small and piercing, and they seemed now to send out a little, deadly jet of venom, as he waited for the boat to come within his grasp.

He seized the point of the bows and jerked the boat roughly towards him, so that its keel rasped on the stones. John drew the oars aboard and laid them neatly under either gunwale. Then he picked up his trout and stepped out onto the shingle.

'Caught you,' said Mike Boyle. 'Caught you at last. Pinching my boat in the early morning to go fishing, thinking I wouldn't spot you. But the early bird catches the worm, and I've caught a worm this morning all right.'

'This is the first time I've borrowed the boat,' said John.

'Borrowing without leave is stealing, young man,' said Mike Boyle. 'Didn't they teach you that at home?' He lifted one side of his upper lip. 'Maybe they didn't, though. You can't teach something if you don't know it yourself.'

Standing silently in front of Mike Boyle, John felt as if a volcano were about to erupt inside him. It seemed as if he had suddenly grown two feet taller, so that he towered in the air over this little man's head, as if he had suddenly become strong enough to lift Mike Boyle by his thick bull neck and send him spinning through the air like a shrieking rainbow, until he landed in the middle of the lake with a splash that would sprinkle the sun. But the volcano died down again and he said:

'My father doesn't know I took the boat.'

'But he'll know when you bring home that trout for his breakfast,' said Mike Boyle. 'And it will be all the sweeter because it was caught from my boat.' He stuck out a hand whose fingers twitched with impatient energy. 'Just give me that fish, young man. That will teach you better than any talk, not to steal my boat again.'

John put the fish behind his back for safety.

'It's my fish,' he said. 'You won't get it. I caught it.'

'You caught it from my boat, so it belongs to me.'

'The fish belongs to the line, not to the boat.'

'You'd never have caught that fish without my boat,' said Mike Boyle contemptuously. 'There's no one knows it better than yourself. That's why you had to get up at the crack of dawn, when you thought everyone would be asleep, and sneak down here like the thief you are.'

If the Jersey heifer had not come rambling down to the edge of the lake just then, John might have held to his resolution of not telling how he had saved her life an hour ago. Now all at once he found that he could no longer bear the injustice of Mike Boyle's accusations. As he began to tell the story, it occurred to him that it might soften Mike Boyle's heart to hear it, as well as making him understand how John had come to borrow the boat. 'Do good to them that hate you,' John's father always said.

While he described how he had led the heifer step by step ashore, he watched Mike Boyle's face, how the eyebrows jerked and lifted, and at last there was even the beginnings of a sour smile. Swinging the fish easily in his left hand, John pointed with his right to the exact place where the heifer had stood. Mike Boyle's eye followed the pointing forefinger, and then dropped quickly, covetously, to the fish. The sour smile became a sour, snorting laugh.

'A little hero,' he said. 'You'd better go over at once, and tell your story to Tom Burge, for I sold him that heifer last week. She's wandered back twice already. Maybe he'll make you a present of the calf as a reward. And now, just hand over that fish without any more talk.'

This time, the twitching hand made a grab for the fish. Instinctively, John lifted it high out of his reach so that it dangled in the air between them. Then it seemed to him that it dwindled in size there before his eyes, that its scales no longer shone with the same lustre, that its soft, ribbed tail had become dry and ugly and stark. He thought of the bad blood, and he saw quite clearly that future generations of his own family and of the Boyles might some day curse this little fish, if he allowed it to stir up still further the ill feeling between them.

Slowly he lowered his arm and stretched it towards Mike

79

Boyle. He could not bring himself to speak. Mike Boyle's little eyes narrowed, but though he put out his hand he did not take the trout at once. He paused for a moment and then snapped at it sharply, like a dog catching a fly. When it was gone, John felt serene and calm, as if he had done Mike Boyle a great service, or as if he had after all been the victor in spite of losing his fish.

Perhaps the same idea came to trouble Mike Boyle's satisfaction. John was astonished to see a look of hurt bewilderment replace the triumphant expression that he had had at the moment of success. Then all at once he was bellowing:

'Get off my land! I'll have the law on you! Get off! Get off!'

Grinning from ear to ear, John skipped under the flimsy wire into his own field, and started to run up the long slope towards home.

Seumas MacManus (1868-1960)
Seumas MacManus was born in County Donegal, the son of a poor
farmer. He became a National School Teacher in the school where he
himself had been taught. He was a prolific writer of stories, verse and
plays, but the retelling of popular folktales was his favourite medium.
'The Widow's Daughter' is from his collection of folktales *Hibernian
Nights* and is a Cinderella story with a difference. Seumas MacManus
lived to be over ninety and died in New York City.

The Widow's Daughter
Seumas MacManus

THERE WAS ONCE A POOR WIDOW WOMAN, living in Donegal,
with a daughter Nabla, who grew up both idle and lazy, till,
when she became a young woman, she was both thriftless
and useless, only fit to sit with her heels in the ashes and
croon to the cat the day long. One time, at length, her
mother got so vexed for her refusing to do some trifle about
the house that she got a stick and began thrashing her.

Who should happen to ride by just then but the King's
son; and when he heard the walloping and scolding, and
crying and pleading within, he drew rein and shouted to
know what was the matter. The widow came to the door,
curtseying when she saw who he was, and, not wishing to
put out a bad name on the girl, said that as she had a
daughter who killed herself working, and refused to rest
when her mother commanded, she had to be beaten into
moderating her labour.

'That's surely a strange failing,' says the King's son. 'What
work does your daughter do?'

'Spin, weave, sew, and everything that woman ever did,'
the mother replied.

Now, it so happened that a twelvemonth before the
Prince had taken a notion to marry, and his mother, anxious
that he should wed none but the best, had sent messengers
around Ireland to find a woman who could perform all a
woman's   duties   and   especially   the   very   three

81

accomplishments the widow named; but all candidates who offered were unsatisfactory when put to the test, and the Prince had remained unwedded. So the Prince rejoiced when he heard the widow's charge against Nabla.

'You aren't fit to be mother or have charge of such a remarkable girl,' said he. 'For twelve months my mother has been searching out such a maid to make her my wife. I'll take Nabla with me.'

Nabla was enchanted at this and her mother astonished. The King's son helped Nabla to a seat behind him and, bidding adieu to the widow, rode off.

To his mother, the Queen, he introduced Nabla, telling how by good fortune he had found the very woman they had so long looked for in vain. This wonderful girl could spin, weave and sew, and do everything else a woman should, and moreover was so eager for work that her mother was flailing her within an inch of her life to make her stop working when he arrived on the scene. The Queen said that was well. But she'd put her to the test anyway.

She took Nabla to a room where was a heap of raw silk and a silver wheel, and told her to have all the silk spun into thread before night – then left, locking the door after.

Poor Nabla, dumbfounded, sat staring at the big heap of silk and the silver wheel till at length she began to cry. For she had never spun a yard of thread in all her life long.

Very soon an ugly old woman, with one of her feet as big as a bolster, appeared. 'For what are you crying?' she asked Nabla.

Nabla told her, and the old hag said, 'I'll spin the silk for you if you promise to bid me to the wedding.'

'I do that with heart and a half,' Nabla said. And the old woman sat to the wheel, and, working it with the big foot, spun the heap in less than no time.

When the Queen came and found all spun she said, 'That is good.' Next day she gave Nabla a golden loom and told Nabla she must have all the thread woven in webs before night. And locking the door, she left Nabla looking, distracted, from the thread to the loom, and from the loom to the thread – for she hadn't, in her life, once thrown a shuttle. At length she laid her face in her hands and began to cry.

82

Soon there appeared an ugly old woman with one hand big as a pot hanging by her side. She asked Nabla why she cried, and Nabla told her. Then the hag said,

'I'll do the weaving for you if you'll promise to bid me to your wedding.'

'I'll surely do that, and welcome,' Nabla said.

So the old one sat to the loom and, throwing the shuttle with her great big hand, very soon had all the thread woven in webs.

When the Queen came and found the work done she said, 'That is good.'

Next day she gave Nabla a gold needle and thimble, and said that before night, she must have all the webs made in shirts for the Prince and his friends.

When the Queen had gone, Nabla, who had never even threaded a needle in her life, sat, wildly looking from the needle and thimble to the webs of silk. And again she broke down and began crying her eyes out.

An ugly old hag with monstrous big nose that weighed her head down appeared and asked why she cried.

Nabla told her, and the ugly old one said, 'I'll make the webs into shirts for the Prince if you'll bid me to your wedding.'

'I'll do that,' Nabla said, 'and a thousand welcomes.'

So the old woman, taking the needle and thimble, sat down, and, with her big nose drooping into her work, in short time had all the webs wrought into shirts and disappeared again.

When the Queen came and found all the silk made in shirts, she was mightily pleased and said, 'You are the woman for my son. He'll never need to call in a spinner, a weaver, or a seamstress while you live.'

Then Nabla and the Prince were betrothed, and on the wedding day there was a gay and gorgeous company in the Palace hall. All was mirth and festivity, and everyone past himself or herself with happiness and delight.

Everyone, that is excepting the one who should be happiest of all, Nabla. Instead of being happy her heart was weighted with despair, for thinking of what would happen to her the first time her husband asked her to spin or to weave or to make him a shirt.

As the company seated themselves to the long tables to begin the wedding feast, there came a loud knock on the door at the bottom of the hall, and when a servant opened it, the Prince and all his guests were astonished to behold enter an ugly old hag who, lifting and laying one great big foot, came hirpledy-hop, hirpledy-hop, all the way up the floor to where the Prince sat at the head table with his bride!

When the ugly old hag reached there, the Prince politely arose and bowed to her saying, 'You're welcome, madam, to my wedding. May I ask whose bidding are you?'

And the old hag answered, 'I'm the bride's bidding,'

'Then you're double welcome,' said the Prince, believing she was one of Nabla's poor friends. He ordered room to be made for her by the bride's right hand, and as she sat down, he asked, 'Would you mind, dear madam, telling the company and myself what made your foot so big?' And she answered, 'I've been a lifetime working the spinning wheel with it, till all the blood in my body ran into the foot, leaving me the spectacle you are beholding.'

'Then by my word,' said the Prince, striking the table a great blow, 'my beautiful bride shall never put foot to a wheel while I'm alive to prevent it!' And he ordered the feast to begin.

But as the party would settle to their feasting, a great knock sounded on the door, everyone turned to look, and when a servant opened it, in walked a woman with one hand as big as a stool. The weight of the hand hanging by her side gave her body a monstrous lean-over, so that as she hobbled up the floor, the company at the tables, watching, were silent in surprise.

When she reached him, the Prince politely arose and bowed to her, saying, 'You are welcome to my wedding, madam. May I ask whose bidding are you?'

And the hag answered, 'I'm the bride's bidding.'

'Then you're double welcome,' said the Prince, believing she, too, was one of Nabla's poor friends. He ordered room to be made for her. And as she sat down, he asked, 'Would you mind, dear madam, telling the company and myself what made your hand so big?'

'Weaving,' she answered him. 'I have slaved at the loom, throwing the shuttle all my life, till all the blood in my body ran into the hand, leaving it the spectacle as you see.'

'Then,' said the Prince, striking the table a thundering blow, 'by my word, my wife shall never throw a shuttle again while I live to prevent it. On with the feast,' he said.

But, as the company would begin, a great knock on the door startled them. Everyone turned, and saw the servant admit an ugly old woman with the greatest nose ever beheld or dreamt of! Up the floor she waddled, her weighed head wagging from side to side – up the floor, and up the floor.

When she reached the head table, the Prince politely arose and bowed to her, saying, 'Madam, you're welcome to my wedding. But may I ask whose bidding are you?'

And she answered, 'I'm the bride's bidding.'

'Then you're thrice welcome,' said the Prince, believing she also was one of Nabla's poor friends. He ordered room to be made for her, and as she sat down, he asked, 'Would you mind, dear madam, telling the company and myself what made your nose so big?'

'It's from sewing,' she said. 'All my life I've been stooping my head over shirts a-sewing, till every drop of blood in my body ran down into my nose, making it the monster you're beholding.'

The Prince struck the table a blow that made all the dishes bounce. 'By my word,' he said, 'my wife shall never thread a needle again, or do any other sort of housework while I live to prevent it!'

Nabla's low heart now leapt to hit the roof. At once she was the happiest of the hundreds of happy ones there, and the day that had begun dark and despairful for her turned the very brightest, very joyfullest, of all her life.

The Prince faithfully kept his word. He was always on watch to catch Nabla spinning, weaving, sewing, or doing any kind of work that woman ever did. He even hired spies to report to him if she tried to work in secret.

Nabla, however, never did anything to make him uneasy, but, forgiving her old mother and taking her to live in the castle with her, she ever after lived happy and content and lazy as the day was long.

Jonathan Swift (1667-1745)
Before there was such a thing as children's literature, young people
adopted the story of Gulliver's travels 'into several remote nations of the
world.' This book first appeared more than two hundred and fifty years
ago and it has been enjoyed since then all over the world. Some people
might even forget that its author was an Irishman, Dean of St. Patrick's
Cathedral in Dublin, and one of the first Irish patriots.
The extract below describes Lemuel Gulliver's shipwreck and his first
encounter with the miniature world of Lilliput. Later chapters of the
book tell of his adventures in such strange lands as Brobdingnag (where
everyone is huge), Laputa, and the home of the Houyhnhnms and the
original Yahoos.

Gulliver Reaches Lilliput

Jonathan Swift

An excerpt from *Gulliver's Travels*

WE SET SAIL FROM BRISTOL May 4, 1699, and our voyage at first
was very prosperous.

It would not be proper, for some reasons, to trouble the
reader with the particulars of our adventures in those seas:
let it suffice to inform him, that in our passage from thence
to the East-Indies, we were driven by a violent storm to the
north-west of Van Diemen's Land. By an observation, we
found ourselves in the latitude of 30 degrees 2 minutes
south. Twelve of our crew were dead by immoderate labour
and ill food, the rest were in a very weak condition. On the
fifth of November, which was the beginning of summer in
those parts, the weather being very hazy, the seamen spied
a rock, within half a cable's length of the ship; but the wind
was so strong, that we were driven directly upon it, and
immediately split. Six of the crew, of whom I was one,
having let down the boat into the sea, made a shift to get
clear of the ship, and the rock. We rowed by my
computation about three leagues, till we were able to work
no longer, being already spent with labour while we were in
the ship. We therefore trusted ourselves to the mercy of the

waves, and in about half an hour the boat was overset by a sudden flurry from the north. What became of my companions in the boat, as well as of those who escaped on the rock, or were left in the vessel, I cannot tell; but conclude they were all lost. For my own part, I swam as fortune directed me, and was pushed forward by wind and tide. I often let my legs drop, and could feel no bottom: but when I was almost gone, and able to struggle no longer, I found myself within my depth; and by this time the storm was much abated. The declivity was so small, that I walked near a mile before I got to the shore, which I conjectured was about eight o'clock in the evening. I then advanced forward near half a mile, but could not discover any sign of houses or inhabitants; at least I was in so weak a condition, that I did not observe them. I was extremely tired, and with that, and the heat of the weather, and about half a pint of brandy that I drank as I left the ship, I found myself much inclined to sleep. I lay down on the grass, which was very short and soft, where I slept sounder than ever I remember to have done in my life, and as I reckoned, above nine hours; for when I awaked, it was just day-light. I attempted to rise, but was not able to stir: for, as I happened to lie on my back, I found my arms and legs were strongly fastened on each side to the ground; and my hair, which was long and thick, tied down in the same manner. I likewise felt several slender ligatures across my body, from my armpits to my thighs, I could only look upwards; the sun began to grow hot, and the light offended my eyes. I heard a confused noise about me, but in the posture I lay, could see nothing except the sky. In a little time I felt something alive moving on my left leg, which advancing gently forward over my breast, came almost up to my chin; when bending my eyes downwards as much as I could, I perceived it to be a human creature not six inches high, with a bow and arrow in his hands, and a quiver at his back. In the meantime, I felt at least forty more of the same kind (as I conjectured) following the first. I was in the utmost astonishment, and roared so loud, that they all ran back in a fright; and some of them, as I was afterwards told, were hurt with the falls they got by leaping from my sides upon the ground. However, they soon returned, and one of them, who ventured so far·

as to get a full sight of my face, lifting up his hands and eyes by way of admiration, cried out in a shrill but distinct voice, *Hekinah degul*: the others repeated the same words several times, but I then knew not what they meant. I lay all this while, as the reader may believe, in great uneasiness: at length, struggling to get loose, I had the fortune to break the strings, and wrench out the pegs that fastened my left arm to the ground; for, by lifting it up to my face, I discovered the methods they had taken to bind me, and at the same time, with a violent pull, which gave me excessive pain, I a little loosened the strings that tied down my hair on the left side, so that I was just able to turn my head about two inches. But the creatures ran off a second time, before I could seize them; whereupon there was a great shout in a very shrill accent, and after it ceased, I heard one of them cry aloud, *Tolgo phonac*; when in an instant I felt above an hundred arrows discharged on my left hand, which pricked me like so many needles; and besides they shot another flight into the air, as we do bombs in Europe, whereof many, I suppose, fell on my body (though I felt them not) and some on my face, which I immediately covered with my left hand. When this shower of arrows was over, I fell a groaning with grief and pain, and then striving again to get loose, they discharged another volley larger than the first, and some of them attempted with spears to stick me in the sides; but, by good luck, I had on me a buff jerkin, which they could not pierce. I thought it the most prudent method to lie still, and my design was to continue so till night, when, my left hand being already loose, I could easily free myself: and as for the inhabitants, I had reason to believe I might be a match for the greatest armies they could bring against me, if they were all of the same size with him that I saw. But fortune disposed otherwise of me. When the people observed I was quiet, they discharged no more arrows; but, by the noise I heard, I knew their numbers increased; and about four yards from me, over against my right ear, I heard a knocking for above an hour, like that of people at work; when turning my head that way, as well as the pegs and strings would permit me, I saw a stage erected, about a foot and a half from the ground, capable of holding four of the inhabitants, with two or three ladders to mount it: from whence one of them, who seemed to be a person of quality, made me a long speech, whereof I understood not one syllable. But I should have mentioned, that before the principal person began his oration, he cried out three times, *Langro dehul san* (these words and the former were afterwards repeated and explained to me). Whereupon immediately about fifty of the inhabitants came, and cut the strings that fastened the left side of my head, which gave me the liberty of turning it to the right, and of observing the person and gesture of him that was to speak. He appeared to be of a middle age, and taller than any of the other three who attended him, whereof one was a page that held up his train, and seemed to be somewhat longer than my middle finger; the other two stood one on each side to support him. He acted every part of an orator, and I could observe many periods of threatenings, and others of promises, pity, and kindness. I answered in a few words, but in the most submissive manner, lifting up my left hand and both my eyes to the sun, as calling him for a witness; and being almost famished with hunger, having not eaten a morsel for some hours before I left the ship, I found the demands of nature so strong upon me, that I could not forbear showing my impatience (perhaps against the strict rules of decency) by putting my finger frequently on my mouth, to signify that I wanted food. The *Hurgo* (for so they call a great lord, as I afterwards learnt) understood me very well. He descended from the stage, and commanded that several ladders should be applied to my sides, on which above an hundred of the inhabitants mounted, and walked towards my mouth, laden with baskets full of meat, which had been provided, and sent thither by the King's orders, upon the first intelligence he received of me. I observed there was the flesh of several animals, but could not distinguish them by the taste. There were shoulders, legs, and loins, shaped like those of mutton, and very well dressed, but smaller than the wings of a lark. I ate them by two or three at a mouthful, and took three loaves at a time, about the bigness of musket bullets. They supplied me as they could, showing a thousand marks of wonder and astonishment at my bulk and appetite. I then made another sign that I wanted drink. They found by my eating that a small quantity would not suffice me, and being a most ingenious people, they slung up with great dexterity one of their largest hogsheads, then rolled it towards my hand, and beat out the top; I drank it off at a draught which I might well do, for it did not hold half a pint, and tasted like a small wine of Burgundy, but much more delicious. They brought me a second hogshead, which I drank in the same manner, and made signs for more, but they had none to give me. When I had performed these wonders, they shouted for joy, and danced upon my breast, repeating several times as they did at first, *Hekinah degul.* They made me a sign that I should throw down the two hogsheads, but first warning the people below to stand out of the way, crying aloud, *Borach mivola,* and when they saw the vessels in the air, there was an universal shout of *Hekinah degul.* I confess I was often tempted, while they were passing backwards and forwards on my body, to seize forty or fifty of the first that came in my reach, and dash them against the ground. But the remembrance of what I had felt, which probably might not be the worst they could do, and the promise of honour I made them, for so I interpreted my submissive behaviour, soon drove out these imaginations. Besides, I now considered myself as bound by the laws of hospitality to a people who had treated me with so much expense and magnificence. However, in my thoughts I could not sufficiently wonder at the intrepidity of these diminutive mortals who durst venture to mount and walk upon my body, while one of my hands was at liberty, without trembling at the first sight of so prodigious a creature as I must appear to them. After some time, when they observed that I made no more demands for meat, there appeared before me a person of high rank from his Imperial Majesty. His Excellency, having mounted on the small of my right leg, advanced forwards up to my face, with about a dozen of his retinue. And producing his credentials under the Signet Royal, which he applied close to my eyes, spoke ten minutes, without any signs of anger, but with a kind of determinate resolution; often pointing forwards, which, as I afterwards found, was towards the capital city, about half a mile distant, whither it was agreed by his Majesty in council that I must be conveyed. I answered in few words, but to no purpose, and made a sign with my hand that was loose,

91

putting it to the other (but over his Excellency's head, for fear of hurting him or his train) and then to my own head and body, to signify that I desired my liberty. It appeared that he understood me well enough, for he shook his head by way of disapprobation, and held his hand in a posture to show that I must be carried as a prisoner. However, he made other signs to let me understand that I should have meat and drink enough, and very good treatment. Whereupon I once more thought of attempting to break my bonds, but again, when I felt the smart of their arrows upon my face and hands, which were all in blisters, and many of the darts still sticking in them, and observing likewise that the number of my enemies increased, I gave tokens to let them know that they might do with me what they pleased. Upon this the *Hurgo* and his train withdrew with much civility and cheerful countenances. Soon after I heard a general shout, with frequent repetitions of the words, *Peplom selan*, and I felt great numbers of the people on my left side relaxing the cords to such a degree that I was able to turn upon my right. But before this, they had daubed my face and both my hands with a sort of ointment very pleasant to the smell, which in a few minutes removed all the smart of their arrows. These circumstances, added to the refreshment I had received by their victuals and drink, which were very nourishing, disposed me to sleep. I slept about eight hours, as I was afterwards assured; and it was no wonder, for the physicians, by the Emperor's order, had mingled a sleepy potion in the hogsheads of wine.

It seems that upon the first moment I was discovered sleeping on the ground after my landing, the Emperor had early notice of it by an express; and determined in council that I should be tied in the manner I have related (which was done in the night while I slept), that plenty of meat and drink should be sent me, and a machine prepared to carry me to the capital city.

This resolution perhaps may appear very bold and dangerous, and I am confident would not be imitated by any prince in Europe on the like occasion; however, in my opinion, it was extremely prudent, as well as generous. For supposing these people had endeavoured to kill me with their spears and arrows while I was asleep, I should certainly have awaked with the first sense of smart, which might so far have roused my rage and strength, as to have enabled me to break the strings wherewith I was tied; after which, as they were not able to make resistance, so they could expect no mercy.

These people are most excellent mathematicians, and arrived to a great perfection in mechanics by the countenance and encouragement of the Emperor, who is a renowned patron of learning. This prince hath several machines fixed on wheels for the carriage of trees and other great weights. He often builds his largest men-of-war, whereof some are nine foot long, in the woods where the timber grows, and has them carried on these engines three or four hundred yards to the sea. Five hundred carpenters and engineers were immediately set at work to prepare the greatest engine they had. It was a frame of wood raised three inches from the ground, about seven foot long and four wide, moving upon twenty-two wheels. The shout I heard was upon the arrival of this engine, which it seems set out in four hours after my landing. It was brought parallel to me as I lay. But the principal difficulty was to raise and place me in this vehicle. Eighty poles, each of one foot high, were erected for this purpose, and very strong cords of the bigness of packthread were fastened by hooks to many bandages, which the workmen had girt round my neck, my hands, my body, and my legs. Nine hundred of the strongest men were employed to draw up these cords by many pulleys fastened on the poles, and thus, in less than three hours, I was raised and slung into the engine, and there tied fast. All this I was told, for while the whole operation was performing, I lay in a profound sleep, by the force of that soporiferous medicine infused into my liquor. Fifteen hundred of the Emperor's largest horses, each about four inches and a half high, were employed to draw me towards the metropolis, which, as I said, was half a mile distant.

About four hours after we began our journey, I awaked by a very ridiculous accident; for the carriage being stopped a while to adjust something that was out of order, two or three of the young natives had the curiosity to see how I looked when I was asleep; they climbed up into the engine, and advancing very softly to my face, one of them, an officer in the Guards, put the sharp end of his half-pike a good way up into my left nostril, which tickled my nose like a straw, and made me sneeze violently: whereupon they stole off unperceived, and it was three weeks before I knew the cause of my awaking so suddenly. We made a long march the remaining part of that day, and rested at night with five hundred guards on each side of me, half with torches, and half with bows and arrows, ready to shoot me if I should offer to stir. The next morning at sunrise we continued our march, and arrived within two hundred yards of the city gates about noon. The Emperor, and all his court, came out to meet us; but his great officers would by no means suffer his Majesty to endanger his person by mounting on my body.

At the place where the carriage stopped, there stood an ancient temple, esteemed to be the largest in the whole kingdom, which having been polluted some years before by an unnatural murder, was, according to the zeal of those people, looked on as profane, and therefore had been applied to common uses, and all the ornaments and furniture carried away. In this edifice it was determined I should lodge. The great gate fronting to the north was about four foot high, and almost two foot wide, through which I could easily creep. On each side of the gate was a small window not above six inches from the ground: into that on the left side, the King's smiths conveyed fourscore and eleven chains, like those that hang to a lady's watch in Europe, and almost as large, which were locked to my left leg with six and thirty padlocks. Over against this temple, on t'other side of the great highway, at twenty foot distance, there was a turret at least five foot high. Here the Emperor ascended with many principal lords of his court, to have an opportunity of viewing me, as I was told, for I could not see them. It was reckoned that above an hundred thousand inhabitants came out of the town upon the same errand; and in spite of my guards, I believe there could not be fewer than ten thousand, at several times, who mounted upon my body by the help of ladders. But a proclamation was soon issued to forbid it upon pain of death. When the workmen found it was impossible for me to break loose, they cut all the strings that bound me; whereupon I rose up with as melancholy a disposition as ever I had in my life. But the noise and astonishment of the people at seeing me rise and walk, are not to be expressed. The chains that held my left leg were about two yards long, and gave me not only the liberty of walking backwards and forwards in a semicircle; but, being fixed within four inches of the gate, allowed me to creep in, and lie at my full length in the temple.

Kathleen Fitzpatrick (1872-   )
In almost every village or neighbourhood in Ireland there is someone
whose possessions and wealth are as legendary as his stinginess. How
often do we hear it said of someone that he still has his Confirmation
money? In reality wealthy relatives and neighbours usually turn out to
be a disappointment, but not so Mr. McKeown about whom it was said
that he kept all his money tied up in stockings.
Kathleen Fitzpatrick, the author of this story, was born and educated in
Belfast. The book, from which this extract comes, was first published in
1905 under the title *The Weans of Rowallan* and is the account of the
childhood adventures of a remarkable and eccentric bunch of Edwardian
children who romp through the book as they must have romped
through County Down at the turn of the century, leaving everyone
slightly breathless.

A Stocking Full of Gold
Kathleen Fitzpatrick

MRS. KELLY and her grandson Tom lived in one of the two
cottages just outside the gates. Her husband when he was
alive had worked at Rowallan. She was a sprightly little
woman, rosy-cheeked and black-eyed, and always wore a
black woollen cap that had a border of grey fur round her
face. The children liked to go to tea with her to eat potato
bread, called fadge, hot off the griddle, and to hear the
stories of the days when she was young; when the boys and
girls would walk miles for the sake of a dance, and when
there was not a dance in the countryside that she was not
there to foot it with the best in her muslin dress and white
stockings.

Lull said Mrs. Kelly hadn't her sorrows to seek. But the
children thought they had never seen anybody who looked
more cheerful. She said herself there were not many old
women who were so well off.

'Sure I've got my wee house that I wouldn't change for
the King's palace,' she said one day, 'and my grandson Tom
that never said a wrong word to me. Wouldn't I be the quare
auld witch if I didn't be thanking Almighty God for it?'

96

But one day old Davy, who lived in the next cottage, brought a message from Mrs. Kelly when he came to work, to say Tom was ill. Jane went down to see Mrs. Kelly.

'He's going to die,' she said when she came back, 'and she's sitting by the fire crying her eyes out.'

'Oh, the critter! She's had sorrow enough without that,' said Lull.

'What ails him?' Mick asked.

'He's got consumption and she says – she says she's buried eight of them with it.'

'God help her – it's herself has got the manly heart,' said Lull.

'Maybe he'll get better,' said Patsy.

'He'll niver do that in this world,' Lull said sadly.

'It's just awful,' said Jane, 'she says there's no cure for it. It would break your heart to see her sitting there.'

'I'm sure as anything Doctor Dixey could cure him,' said Fly. 'Didn't he mend Patsy's foot when he hurt it in the threshing machine, and didn't he take those old ulsters out of my throat?'

There was some hope in this, the children thought; and though Lull shook her head, she allowed them to send Andy for Doctor Dixey.

It was late that evening when the doctor came. Lull had promised the children that they might sit up to hear what he said about Tom. When he did come and Lull took him down to Mrs. Kelly's house he stayed nearly an hour. The children were getting sleepy when he came back to the schoolroom.

'Well?' he said, pulling up a chair to the fire, 'so you want me to cure the boy Tom?'

They all nodded.

'I think it could be done,' Dr. Dixey went on, 'but it would cost a deal of money, more than any of us can afford to spend.'

'How much?' Jane asked.

'Ten pounds at least, and then it is only a chance. And the old woman will be left alone – but she'd be that in any case. You see, the only hope for him is to send him abroad to a dry climate; he'll die if he stays here. And when he gets there he will have to stay there, so the grandmother will

miss him just as much as if he –'

'She wouldn't care,' Jane interrupted; 'sure, couldn't he write letters to her if he was alive? and he couldn't do that if he was dead.'

'But the money – where's that to come from?' asked Dr. Dixey.

'We'll just have to find it,' said Mick.

'That's easier said than done,' said Dr. Dixey as he got up to go. 'But I'll look after the boy while he's here, and if you find the money I'll find the ship.'

They sat up for another hour talking it over with Lull. She said it was useless to think of such a lot of money, but the children declared they must find it somewhere.

After they had gone to bed Jane heard a whispering in the corner of the dark room.

'Who's that?' she said, starting up in bed.

'It's only me saying my prayers,' said Honeybird.

'You said them before I put out the candle. Get back into bed and be quiet.'

Honeybird got into bed, but in about three minutes she was out again.

'What's the matter now?' said Jane.

'It's only me saying my prayers,' Honeybird answered.

'Sure you have said them twice already,' said Jane.

'I'm saying them three times for luck,' said Honeybird as she got back into her bed.

Next morning Mick and Jane started off together to look for the money. Soon after they had left the house Honeybird came into the kitchen.

'Don't you be frightened,' she said, when Lull was tying the strings of her hood; 'I'll be away a good long time but I'll bring something nice when I come back.'

An hour later she was knocking at the door of a big white house nearly two miles away where old Mr. McKeown lived.

None of the children had ever been there before, but they had heard about Mr. McKeown from Teresa, who went there once a week to do his washing. She had told them stories of how he lived all by himself with not even a servant to look after him, and kept all his money tied up in stockings.

99

Honeybird's heart was full of joy. Last night she had asked Almighty God to let her find the money for Tom Kelly to be cured, and when she got back into bed for the last time Almighty God had reminded her that old Mr. McKeown had stockings full of gold.

After rapping for a long time on the panels of the front door – she could not reach the knocker – she walked round to the back of the house and knocked there. But still there was no answer. Then she tried the side door. By this time her knuckles were sore; so, as she found she could turn the handle, she opened the door and walked in. A long passage led to the hall, where she stopped and looked round. There were doors on every side, but they were all shut. The first door she opened showed another passage; the second led into a dark room. But when she opened the third door she saw an old man sitting in an armchair by a fire. Then she shut the door carefully behind her and went up to him, holding out her hand.

'And how are you, Mr. McKeown?' she said.

A bony hand closed over hers for a second, but Mr. McKeown did not speak.

'I hurted my hand rapping on the doors,' she said, 'so I just walked in at last.'

'May I ask who you are?' said Mr. McKeown in a thin voice.

'I'm Honeybird Darragh,' she said.

'Darragh?' he repeated, 'ah, yes.'

Honeybird's eyes wandered round the room. Cupboards with glass doors lined the walls, and the cupboards were full of china.

'May I look at those things?' she asked.

'Certainly, certainly,' said Mr. McKeown.

She got off her chair and walked round the room. In one cupboard there were china ladies and gentlemen in beautiful clothes. She sighed over these.

'Och, I wish I was a lady,' she said; 'wouldn't you like to have long hair, Mr. McKeown?'

'I am afraid it would not afford me much pleasure,' he said.

Honeybird looked at him again. He was very thin and his long back was bent.

100

'Aren't you feared to live here all by yourself?' she asked.

'Afraid? What should I be afraid of?' he asked.

'I'm feared,' she said, 'and there's me and Fly and Patsy and Mick and Jane and Lull and Mother – all those, but I'm feared to death sometimes.'

'What are you afraid of?' he asked.

'I'm feared of ghosts and kidnappers and Skyan the Bugler and the Buggyboo and the Banshee – and when I'm a bad girl I'm awful feared of the devil.'

'Surely that is a rare occurrence?' said Mr. McKeown.

Honeybird did not understand. 'Aren't you afraid of these things?' she asked.

'Not in the least,' he replied.

'Aren't you afraid robbers will come and steal all your stockings full of gold?'

'My stockings full of gold?' he repeated, looking puzzled.

'Teresa says you have heaps and heaps of them,' she said.

'I am afraid they only exist in Teresa's imagination. I have not got one stocking full of gold.'

Honeybird stared at him.

'Then you haven't got one to give away?'

Mr. McKeown sat back in his chair and made a crackling noise in his throat that grew more and more distinct till at last Honeybird realised that he was laughing.

'I have not laughed for ten years,' he said, smiling at her.

She tried to smile back, but her eyes were full of tears.

'Did you expect me to give you a stocking full of gold?'

''Deed I did. I was told to come and ask you for it.'

Mr. McKeown frowned. 'Ah,' he said, 'so it was not simplicity?'

'No, it was a heap of money,' she said.

'Perhaps you can tell me the exact sum?'

'Indeed I can – it was just ten pounds.'

'Ten pounds? What madness! And pray is it to build a new chapel or to convert the Jews that you have been sent to beg for such a sum?'

'It was just to make Tom Kelly well,' she said, tears running down her cheeks. 'He's going to die, and Mrs. Kelly has buried eight of them, and Jane says her heart is broke, and Dr. Dixey said ten pounds would cure him.'

Mr. McKeown coughed. 'Did Dr. Dixey send you to beg

101

for this money?'

She shook her head.

'Perhaps it was Father Ryan or Mr. Rannigan?'

Again she shook her head.

'Was it your sister?'

''Deed it was not, for she just hates you. She says you are a skinflint.'

'I am sorry my conduct does not meet with her approval. But I shall be glad if you tell me to whom I am indebted for the honour of your visit?'

Honeybird looked at him. She did not understand what he meant.

'Who sent you here?' he said.

'Almighty God told me to come,' she said.

'Almighty God!' he said. 'I do not understand.'

'I asked Him to let me find the money to cure Tom Kelly, and I said my prayers three times for luck, and when I was getting back into bed after the third time Almighty God said in a wee whisper, "Old Mr. McKeown's the boy." ' Her disappointment was so bitter that she couldn't stop crying.

'Did you tell this to anyone?' Mr. McKeown asked.

'I didn't tell a soul. I got Lull to tie on my Sunday hood, and came here as quick as quick as I could walk.'

For some time neither of them spoke. Mr. McKeown was walking up and down the room. Honeybird was sniffing and wiping her eyes on her pinafore. At last Mr. McKeown came back to his chair.

'Will you tell it to me all over again?' he said.

'I'll tell you all from the start,' she said.

'Jane said Tom Kelly was going to die, and Fly said Dr. Dixey could cure him because he took the ulsters out of her sore throat. And Dr. Dixey came, and said he: "I can make him better with ten pounds, and if you can find the money I'll find the ship." '

'What is the matter with this Tom?'

'He's got consumption. And we thought and thought, and Jane asked Lull to pawn our Sunday clothes, and Lull said they weren't worth more than a pound. And when I went to bed I prayed like anything and Almighty God told me to come here.' She got up and held out her hand. 'I may as well be saying goodbye to you, Mr. McKeown.'

Mr. McKeown took her hand but did not let it go.

'Perhaps Almighty God did not tell you to come to me,' he said.

'Indeed He did,' she said, trying to swallow a sob; 'but maybe He was just making fun of me.'

'Certainly I have not got stockings full of gold,' Mr. McKeown said.

'Well, I was thinking you had,' she said.

'Ten pounds,' he murmured looking into the fire. Then he got up from his chair. 'Will you wait here till I come back?' he said, and went out of the room.

Honeybird sat down. Her heart was heavy. She had pictured to herself how she would go home with the stocking full of gold, and how glad the others would be when they saw the money and knew that Tom Kelly could be cured. But now she must go back empty handed.

Mr. McKeown was gone such a long time that she was tired of waiting and got up to go home. But before she reached the door it opened and he came in. He had something in his hand.

'Come here,' he said. And to her astonishment he laid on the table a handful of glittering gold pieces. 'That is ten pounds,' he said.

Honeybird looked bewildered.

'It is for you if you will take it.'

She answered by throwing her arms round his legs and hugging them tight. Mr. McKeown took her hand and went back to his chair.

'And what made you say you had none, you old ruffian?' she said, hugging him round the neck this time till he had to beg to be allowed to breathe.

'I think you had better ask Dr. Dixey to call here for it,' he said.

Honeybird's face fell. 'Sure I could take it home myself.'

'I am afraid you might lose it.'

'How could I lose it? Are you feared I'd drop it?' she said. 'But I'll tell you what, I couldn't drop it if you put it in a stocking for me.'

Mr. McKeown smiled. 'Perhaps a sock would do.' He went out of the room again and came back with a sock. 'But it will not be full,' he said, as he tied the money in the toe.

Then he said he would walk home with her.

Honeybird went with him to get his coat, and brushed his top hat for him with her arm as Andy Graham had taught her to brush his. Then they set out hand in hand, Honeybird carrying the sock. Mr. McKeown walked very slowly and Honeybird talked all the way. She told him about her mother and Lull, Andy Graham and old Davy, what she played, and what the others did till they came to the gates of Rowallan.

'Now I must leave you,' Mr. McKeown said.

She kissed him goodbye, and when half-way up the avenue she turned to look back he was gone.

The others were at dinner. Jane and Mick had come back from school. Honeybird ran into the schoolroom waving the sock.

'You were queer and cross with me for getting out of bed last night, weren't you, Janie? But look what it got me!' She shook the gold out of the stocking on to the table.

They danced round her as she told her tale. Honeybird was the least excited of them all. Not even when Dr. Dixey came and made her tell her adventures twice over did she lose her head.

'Sure, Almighty God always does anything I ask Him,' she said. 'Mind you, He's very obliging; if I lose anything He finds it for me as quick as quick.'

'Well, He worked a miracle for you this time,' said Dr. Dixey.

Seán O'Faoláin (1900–1991)
When we finish reading the following story, what we remember most is
not the people or what they say, but the mood and atmosphere of the place in
which the trout was stranded. This was Seán O'Faoláin's special gift.
Seán O'Faoláin was born in Cork in 1900. He has written stories and novels as well
as biographies of Daniel O'Connell and Eamon de Valera. In 1940 he founded a
magazine called The Bell which encouraged many Irish writers.

The Trout
Seán O'Faoláin

ONE OF THE FIRST PLACES Julia always ran to when they arrived
in G— was The Dark Walk. It is a laurel walk, very old;
almost gone wild; a lofty midnight tunnel of smooth, sinewy
branches. Underfoot the tough brown leaves are never dry
enough to crackle: there is always a suggestion of damp and
cool trickle.

She raced right into it. For the first few yards she always
had the memory of the sun behind her, then she felt the
dusk closing swiftly down on her so that she screamed with
pleasure and raced on to reach the light at the far end; and it
was always just a little too long in coming so that she
emerged gasping, clasping her hands, laughing, drinking in
the sun. When she was filled with the heat and glare she
would turn and consider the ordeal again.

This year she had the extra joy of showing it to her small
brother, and of terrifying him as well as herself. And for him
the fear lasted longer because his legs were so short and she
had gone out at the far end while he was still screaming and
racing.

When they had done this many times they came back to
the house to tell everybody that they had done it. He
boasted. She mocked. They squabbled.

'Cry babby!'

'You were afraid yourself, so there!'

'I won't take you any more.'

'You're a big pig.'

'I hate you.'

Tears were threatening, so somebody said, 'Did you see the well?' She opened her eyes at that and held up her long lovely neck suspiciously and decided to be incredulous. She was twelve and at that age little girls are beginning to suspect most stories: they have already found out too many, from Santa Claus to the stork. How could there be a well! In The Dark Walk? That she had visited year after year? Haughtily she said, 'Nonsense.'

But she went back, pretending to be going somewhere else, and she found a hole scooped in the rock at the side of the walk, choked with damp leaves, so shrouded by ferns that she uncovered it only after much searching. At the back of this little cavern there was about a quart of water. In the water she suddenly perceived a panting trout. She rushed for Stephen and dragged him to see, and they were both so excited that they were no longer afraid of the darkness as they hunched down and peered in at the fish panting in his tiny prison, his silver stomach going up and down like an engine.

Nobody knew how the trout got there. Even old Martin in the kitchen garden laughed and refused to believe that it was there, or pretended not to believe, until she forced him to come down and see. Kneeling and pushing back his tattered old cap he peered in.

'Be cripes, you're right. How the divil in hell did that fella get there?'

She stared at him suspiciously.

'You knew?' she accused; but he said, 'The divil a' know,' and reached down to lift it out. Convinced, she hauled him back. If she had found it, then it was her trout.

Her mother suggested that a bird had carried the spawn. Her father thought that in the winter a small streamlet might have carried it down there as a baby, and it had been safe until the summer came and the water began to dry up. She said, 'I see,' and went back to look again and consider the matter in private. Her brother remained behind, wanting to hear the whole story of the trout, not really interested in the actual trout but much interested in the story which his mummy began to make up for him on the lines of, 'So one day Daddy Trout and Mammy Trout...' When he retailed it to her she said, 'Pooh.'

It troubled her that the trout was always in the same position; he had no room to turn; all the time the silver belly went up and down; otherwise he was motionless. She wondered what he ate, and in between visits to Joey Pony and the boat, and a bathe to get cool, she thought of his hunger. She brought him down bits of dough; once she brought him a worm. He ignored the food. He just went on panting. Hunched over him she thought how all the winter, while she was at school, he had been in there. All the winter, in The Dark Walk, all day, all night, floating around alone. She drew the leaf of her hat down around her ears and chin and stared. She was still thinking of it as she lay in bed.

It was late June, the longest days of the year. The sun had sat still for a week, burning up the world. Although it was after ten o'clock it was still bright and still hot. She lay on her back under a single sheet, with her long legs spread, trying to keep cool. She could see the D of the moon through the fir tree – they slept on the ground floor. Before they went to bed her mummy had told Stephen the story of the trout again, and she, in her bed, had resolutely presented her back to them and read her book. But she had kept one ear cocked.

'And so, in the end, this naughty fish who would not stay at home got bigger and bigger and bigger, and the water got smaller and smaller....'

Passionately she had whirled and cried, 'Mummy, don't make it a horrible old moral story!' Her mummy had brought in a fairy godmother then, who sent lots of rain, and filled the well, and a stream poured out and the trout floated away down to the river below. Staring at the moon she knew that there are no such things as fairy godmothers and that the trout, down in The Dark Walk, was panting like an engine. She heard somebody unwind a fishing reel. Would the *beasts* fish him out!

She sat up. Stephen was a hot lump of sleep, lazy thing. The Dark Walk would be full of little scraps of moon. She leaped up and looked out the window, and somehow it was

108

not so lightsome now that she saw the dim mountains far away and the black firs against the breathing land and heard a dog say *bark-bark*. Quietly she lifted the ewer of water and climbed out the window and scuttled along the cool but cruel gravel down to the maw of the tunnel. Her pyjamas were very short so that when she splashed water it wet her ankles. She peered into the tunnel. Something alive rustled inside there. She raced in, and up and down she raced, and flurried, and cried aloud, 'Oh, gosh, I can't find it,' and then at last she did. Kneeling down in the damp she put her hand into the slimy hole. When the body lashed they were both mad with fright. But she gripped him and shoved him into the ewer and raced, with her teeth ground, out to the other end of the tunnel and down the steep paths to the river's edge.

All the time she could feel him lashing his tail against the side of the ewer. She was afraid he would jump right out. The gravel cut into her soles until she came to the cool ooze of the river's bank where the moon mice on the water crept into her feet. She poured out, watching until he plopped. For a second he was visible in the water. She hoped he was not dizzy. Then all she saw was the glimmer of the moon in the silent-flowing river, the dark firs, the dim mountains, and the radiant pointed face laughing down at her out of the empty sky.

She scuttled up the hill, in the window, plonked down the ewer, and flew through the air like a bird into bed. The dog said *bark-bark*. She heard the fishing reel whirring. She hugged herself and giggled. Like a river of joy her holiday spread before her.

In the morning Stephen rushed to her, shouting that 'he' was gone, and asking 'where' and 'how'. Lifting her nose in the air she said superciliously, 'Fairy godmother, I suppose?' and strolled away patting the palms of her hands.

Frances Browne (1816-1879)
Long before Hans Christian Andersen or Oscar Wilde were writing their
original fairy stories, Frances Browne had invented her most famous
story *Granny's Wonderful Chair and its Tales of Fairy Times*.The idea is
splendid – that a child can sit in a chair and say 'Chair of my
grandmother, tell me a story'.
Frances Browne was born on 16 January 1816 in Donegal, where her
father was postmaster. She was the seventh in a family of twelve
children and was blind from infancy as a result of an attack of smallpox.
Her brothers and sisters taught her stories, many of them old Irish folk
and fairy tales. Eventually she began to write herself, and her first poem
was published in *The Irish Penny Journal*. Today her poetry is almost
forgotten, but *Granny's Wonderful Chair* has been reprinted many times
and continues to enchant with its stories of Snowflower and Dame
Frostyface.

Granny's Wonderful Chair

Frances Browne

IN AN OLD TIME, LONG AGO, when the fairies were in the
world, there lived a little girl so uncommonly fair and
pleasant of look, that they called her Snowflower. This girl
was good as well as pretty. No one had ever seen her frown
or heard her say a cross word, and young and old were glad
when they saw her coming.

Snowflower had no relation in the world but a very old
grandmother, called Dame Frostyface. People did not like
her quite so well as her granddaughter, for she was cross
enough at times, but always kind to Snowflower; and they
lived together in a little cottage built of peat, and thatched
with reeds, on the edge of a great forest; tall trees sheltered
its back from the north wind; the midday sun made its front
warm and cheerful; swallows built in the eaves; daisies grew
thick at the door; but there were none in all that country
poorer than Snowflower and her grandmother. A cat and
two hens were all their livestock; their bed was dry grass,
and the only good piece of furniture in the cottage was a
great arm-chair with wheels on its feet, a black velvet

cushion, and many curious carvings of flowers and fawns on its dark oaken back.

On that chair Dame Frostyface sat spinning from morning till night to maintain herself and her granddaughter, while Snowflower gathered sticks for firing, looked after the hens and the cat, and did whatever else her grandmother bade her. There was nobody in the shire could spin such fine yarn as Dame Frostyface, but she spun very slowly. Her wheel was as old as herself, and far the more worn; indeed, the wonder was that it did not fall to pieces. So the dame's earnings were small, and their living meagre. Snowflower, however, felt no want of good dinners or fine clothes. Every evening, when the fire was heaped with the sticks she had gathered till it blazed and crackled up the cottage chimney, Dame Frostyface set aside her wheel, and told her a new story. Often did the little girl wonder where her grandmother had gathered so many stories, but she soon learned that. One sunny morning, at the time of the swallows coming, the dame rose up, put on the grey hood and mantle in which she carried her yarn to the fairs, and said: 'My child, I am going a long journey to visit an aunt of mine, who lives far in the north country. I cannot take you with me, because my aunt is the crossest woman alive, and never liked young people; but the hens will lay eggs for you; there is barley-meal in the barrel; and, as you have been a good girl, I'll tell you what to do when you feel lonely. Lay your head gently down on the cushion of the arm-chair, and say: "Chair of my grandmother, tell me a story." It was made by a cunning fairy, who lived in the forest when I was young, and she gave it to me because she knew nobody could keep what they got hold of better. Remember, you must never ask a story more than once in a day; and if there be any occasion to travel, you only have to seat yourself in it, and say: "Chair of my grandmother, take me such a way." It will carry you wherever you wish; but mind to oil the wheels before you set out, for I have sat on it these forty years in that same corner.'

Having said this, Dame Frostyface set forth to see her aunt in the north country. Snowflower gathered firing, and looked after the hens and cat as usual. She baked herself a cake or two of the barley-meal; but when the evening fell the cottage looked lonely. Then Snowflower remembered her grandmother's words, and laying her head gently down, she said: 'Chair of my grandmother, tell me a story.'

Scarce were the words spoken, when a clear voice from under the velvet cushion began to tell a new and most wonderful tale, which surprised Snowflower so much that she forgot to be frightened. After that the good girl was lonely no more. Every morning she baked a barley cake, and every evening the chair told her a new story but she could never find out who owned the voice, though Snowflower showed her gratitude by polishing up the oaken back, and dusting the velvet cushion, till the chair looked as good as new. The swallows came and built in the eaves, the daisies grew thicker than ever at the door; but great misfortunes fell upon Snowflower. Notwithstanding all her care, she forgot to clip the hens' wings, and they flew away one morning to visit their friends, the pheasants, who lived far in the forest; the cat followed them to see its relations; the barley-meal was eaten up, except a couple of handfuls; and Snowflower had often strained her eyes in hopes of seeing the grey mantle, but there was no appearance of Dame Frostyface.

'My grandmother stays long,' said Snowflower to herself; 'and by-and-by there will be nothing to eat. If I could get to her, perhaps she would advise me what to do; and this is a good occasion for travelling.'

Next day, at sunrise, Snowflower oiled the chair's wheels, baked a cake out of the last of the meal, took it in her lap by way of provision for the journey, seated herself, and said: 'Chair of my grandmother, take me the way she went.'

Presently the chair gave a creak, and began to move out of the cottage and into the forest the very way Dame Frostyface had taken, where it rolled along at the rate of a coach-and-six. Snowflower was amazed at this style of travelling, but the chair never stopped nor stayed the whole summer day, till as the sun was setting they came upon an open space, where a hundred men were hewing down the tall trees with their axes, a hundred more were cleaving them for firewood, and twenty wagoners, with horses and wagons, were carrying the wood away. 'Oh, chair of my grandmother, stop!' said Snowflower, for she was tired, and also wished to know what this might mean. The chair immediately stood still, and Snowflower, seeing an old wood-cutter, who looked civil, stepped up to him, and said: 'Good father, tell me why you cut all this wood?'

'What ignorant country girl are you?' replied the man, 'not to have heard of the great feast which our sovereign, King Winwealth, means to give on the birthday of his only daughter, the Princess Greedalind. It will last seven days. Everybody will be feasted, and this wood is to roast the oxen and the sheep, the geese and the turkeys, among which there is a great lamentation throughout the land.'

When Snowflower heard that, she could not help wishing to see, and perhaps share in, such a noble feast, after living so long on barley cakes; so, seating herself, she said: 'Chair of my grandmother, take me quickly to the palace of King Winwealth.'

The words were hardly spoken, when off the chair started through the trees and out of the forest, to the great amazement of the wood-cutters, who, never having seen such a sight before, threw down their axes, left their wagons, and followed Snowflower to the gates of a great and splendid city, fortified with strong walls and high towers, and standing in the midst of a wide plain covered with corn-fields, orchards and villages.

It was the richest city in all the land; merchants from every quarter came there to buy and sell, and there was a saying that people had only to live seven years in it to make their fortunes. Rich as they were, however, Snowflower thought she had never seen so many discontented, covetous faces as looked out from the great shops, grand houses and fine coaches, when her chair rattled along the streets; indeed, the citizens did not stand high in repute for either good-nature or honesty; but it had not been so when King Winwealth was young, and he and his brother, Prince Wisewit, governed the land together – Wisewit was a wonderful prince for knowledge and prudence. He knew the whole art of government, the tempers of men, and the powers of the stars; moreover, he was a great magician, and it was said of him that he could never die or grow old. In his time there was neither discontent nor sickness in the city – strangers were hospitably entertained without price or questions. Lawsuits there were none, and no one locked his door at night. The fairies used to come there at May-day and Michaelmas, for they were Prince Wisewit's friends – all but one, called Fortunetta, a shortsighted, but very cunning, fairy, who hated everybody wiser than herself, and the prince especially, because she could never deceive him.

There was peace and pleasure for many a year in King Winwealth's city, till one day at midsummer Prince Wisewit went alone to the forest, in search of a strange herb for his garden, but he never came back; and though the king, with all his guards, searched far and near, no news was ever heard of him. When his brother was gone, King Winwealth grew lonely in his great palace, so he married a certain princess, called Wantall, and brought her home to be his queen. This princess was neither handsome nor agreeable. People thought she must have gained the king's love by enchantment, for her whole dowry was a desert island, with a huge pit in it that never could be filled, and her disposition was so covetous, that the more she got the greedier she grew. In process of time the king and queen had an only daughter, who was to be the heiress of all their dominions. Her name was the Princess Greedalind, and the whole city was making preparations to celebrate her birthday – not that they cared much for the princess, who was remarkably like her mother both in looks and temper, but, being King Winwealth's only daughter, people came from far and near to the festival, and among them strangers and fairies who had not been there since the days of Prince Wisewit.

There was surprising bustle about the palace, a most noble building, so spacious that it had a room for every day in the year. All the floors were of ebony, and all the ceilings of silver, and there was such a supply of golden dishes used by the household, that five hundred armed men kept guard night and day lest any of them should be stolen. When these guards saw Snowflower and her chair, they ran one after another to tell the king, for the like had never been seen nor heard of in his dominions, and the whole court crowded out to see the little maiden and her chair that came of itself.

When Snowflower saw the lords and ladies in their embroidered robes and splendid jewels, she began to feel ashamed of her own bare feet and linen gown; but at length, taking courage, she answered all their questions, and told them everything about her wonderful chair. The queen and the princess cared for nothing that was not gilt. The courtiers had learned the same fashion, and all turned away in high disdain except the old king, who, thinking the chair might amuse him sometimes when he got out of spirits, allowed Snowflower to stay and feast with the scullion in his worst kitchen. The poor little girl was glad of any quarters, though nobody made her welcome – even the servants despised her bare feet and linen gown. They would give her chair no room but in a dusty corner behind the back door, where Snowflower was told she might sleep at night, and eat up the scraps the cook threw away.

That very day the feast began. It was fine to see the multitudes of coaches and people on foot and on horseback who crowded to the palace, and filled every room according to their rank. Never had Snowflower seen such roasting and boiling. There was wine for the lords and spiced ale for the common people, music and dancing of all kinds, and the best of gay dresses; but with all the good cheer there seemed little merriment, and a deal of ill-humour in the palace.

Some of the guests thought they should have been feasted in grander rooms; others were vexed to see many finer than themselves. All the servants were dissatisfied because they did not get presents. There was somebody caught every hour stealing the cups, and a multitude of people were always at the gates clamouring for goods and lands, which Queen Wantall had taken from them. The guards continually drove them away, but they came back again, and could be heard plainly in the highest banquet hall; so it was not wonderful that the old king's spirits got uncommonly low that evening after supper. His favourite page, who always stood behind him, perceiving this, reminded His Majesty of the little girl and her chair.

'It is a good thought,' said King Winwealth. 'I have not heard a story this many a year. Bring the child and the chair instantly!'

The favourite page sent a messenger to the first kitchen, who told the master-cook, the master-cook told the kitchen-maid, the kitchen-maid told the chief scullion, the chief

116

scullion told the dust-boy, and he told Snowflower to wash her face, rub up her chair, and go to the highest banquet hall, for the great King Winwealth wished to hear a story.

Nobody offered to help her, but when Snowflower had made herself as smart as she could with soap and water, and rubbed the chair till it looked as if dust had never fallen on it, she seated herself, and said: 'Chair of my grandmother, take me to the highest banquet hall.'

Instantly the chair marched in a grave and courtly fashion out of the kitchen, up the grand staircase, and into the highest hall. The chief lords and ladies of the land were entertained there, besides many fairies and notable people from distant countries. There had never been such company in the palace since the time of Prince Wisewit; nobody wore less than embroidered satin. King Winwealth sat on his ivory throne in a robe of purple velvet, stiff with flowers of gold; the queen sat by his side in a robe of silver cloth, clasped with pearls; but the Princess Greedalind was finer still, the feast being in her honour. She wore a robe of cloth of gold, clasped with diamonds; two waiting-ladies in white satin stood one on either side, to hold her fan and handkerchief; and two pages, in gold-lace livery, stood behind her chair. With all that, Princess Greedalind looked ugly and spiteful; she and her mother were angry to see a barefooted girl and an old chair allowed to enter the banquet hall.

The supper-table was still covered with golden dishes and the best of good things, but no one offered Snowflower a morsel; so, having made a humble courtesy to the king, the queen, the princess and the good company, most of whom scarcely noticed her, the poor little girl sat down upon the carpet, laid her head on the velvet cushion, as she used to do in the old cottage, and said: 'Chair of my grandmother, tell me a story.'

117

Pádraic Ó Conaire (1882-1928)
Pádraic Ó Conaire was born in Galway in 1882. In 1914 he gave up his
job in the Civil Service to wander the roads of Ireland with a donkey and
cart, and to devote his life to writing. 'M'Asal Beag Dubh' is his most
famous story and has been translated into English especially for this
book by Máirín Ní Dhonnchadha.
Pádraic Ó Conaire died in the Richmond Hospital in Dublin on
6 October 1928, practically destitute – his pipe, tobacco and an apple
were his sole possessions. Five years later a monument was erected in
his honour in Eyre Square, Galway.

My Little Black Ass
Pádraic Ó Conaire

A translation from the Irish by Máirín Ní Dhonnchadha
of *M'Asal Beag Dubh*

IN KINVARA I WAS WHEN FIRST I got to know my little black ass.
It was a fair-day and he was standing there by the ditch, his
backside to the wind, unconcerned with the world and the
world unconcerned with him.

But I was interested in him from the start. I wanted an ass,
I was tired of walking – wouldn't he carry me and my bag,
my overcoat and everything? And who knows but maybe
I'd get him cheaply enough?

I enquired for his owner, but I had to search the town
before I found him. He was outside a public house, singing
for pennies. By Christ! He'd sell the ass. Why wouldn't he if
he got the value of him? Yes, his value; not a single penny
did he want but his value; and of course, only that he'd had
such hardship he'd never part with him – no, never! A fine
young ass who could easily do twenty miles a day. If he got
a handful of oats, once a month, there wouldn't be a
racehorse in the country to keep pace with him – devil a
horse!

We both went to look at the ass. The praise the travelling
man gave him! There had never been an ass, since the first

118

ass came to Ireland, so spirited, so sensible, so far-sighted –

'Do you know a habit he has?' he said admiringly, 'if you gave him a fist of oats in the morning, he'd put some of it aside for fear that it would be scarce the following day. By all the holy books in Rome he would!'

Somebody laughed. The travelling man turned on him. 'What are you laughing at, you half-wit?' said the travelling man. 'He's that sensible that he puts a share of his oats aside; wasn't I often so short myself that I had to steal some from him – only for that ass it's often that I myself and my twelve daughters would have gone hungry....'

I asked him whether he'd distinguish between the neighbour's portion and his master's.

'He's as honest as the priest,' the fellow said, 'if every other beast was like him there'd be no call for ditch or fence, wall or dyke – no call whatsoever.'

A large crowd had gathered around us by this time. His own family was there – I don't know whether the whole twelve of them were present, but as for those that were –you wouldn't meet in any other place in Ireland a more ragged, dirty, greasy pack of children than they, each one more bad-mannered than the next. His wife was there, barefooted, bareheaded, wild ....

She put in her spake.

'Do you remember the day, Peter,' said she to her husband, 'the day that he went in swimming into the river and rescued poor Mickeleen who was being carried away by the current?'

'Why wouldn't I remember it?' said he, 'yes indeed, Sive, and the day I was offered five pounds for him –'

'Five pounds,' said she to me, 'five pounds he got for him, five yellow sovereigns into his hand –'

'Upon my soul I did,' said he, interrupting her, 'I had the money there in my fist, and the bargain made –'

'But when he saw the poor ass,' said she, 'in tears that we were parting with him, what could he do but renege on the bargain?'

'Quiet,' said he, 'speak softly, I say! There's not a word that we're saying that he doesn't understand. Look at his ear cocked!'

I offered a pound for this marvellous beast.

'A pound!' shrieked the travelling man.

'A pound!' said his wife.

'A pound!' said the twelve daughters in unison.

How astounded they all were! They gathered round me, scrutinising me with wide eyes. One child took hold of my coat, another took hold of my trousers, the youngest held onto my knee. Another one of them put a hand in my trouser-pocket: of course, the poor creature was only checking to see if I had the pound itself – but it wasn't a pound he got but a box on the ear and not from the gentleman of the roads either!

I liked the little black ass well. He'd serve my purpose. He'd carry me part of the road. And I could sell him when I'd grown tired of him.

'A pound,' I repeated.

'Two pounds,' said the travelling man.

'Oh woe! woe!' said the wife, 'my fine ass sold for two pounds!' and she began to wail tearfully.

'For a pound,' said I.

'For a pound – and sixpence apiece to the children.' That was the bargain we struck. I gave him the pound. I gave sixpence to each one of his family around me. Then his wife began to call on Johneen and Eameen and Tomeen and I don't know how many more. There wasn't a beggar at the fair but brought his children to me, all of them threatening and clamouring. The noise they made! The confusion, the commotion and the hullabaloo all around me! One saying that he didn't get a single penny, while hiding the shining sixpence under his tongue! Another saying – but you couldn't tell what anyone was saying, or trying to say, with the bedlam around me.

I regretted that I hadn't given him the two pounds to start with, and not bothered with the tips!

I left the town in great style. I was seated on the ass's back, the travelling man gripping the halter on my right, his wife gripping it on my left, the flock of children surrounding us shouting their heads off.

Some of the lads of the town followed us, each one of them with his own advice for me. The ass was compared to the most celebrated racehorses of the day. I was told to take care or he'd take to his heels and never be seen again; I was advised to give him this food and that food – you'd imagine that the sight of myself on my little black ass, escorted by the travelling folk, was the greatest laugh they'd ever had!

But what did I care? Hadn't I the ass, having wanted such a four-footed beast for many a day?

Is it possible to describe how the ass and I parted company with the travellers? Every one of them shook hands with me, nine times over; they all spoke to the ass, softly, calmly, flatteringly, coaxingly.... His traits were recounted for me repeatedly, seven times. I was made promise to be kind and affectionate towards him, to give him a little fistful of oats whenever I could, to favour him with a morsel of hay at night and, on my word, never to use a stick on him....

Then, as we parted, the lament was raised. The father began it. The mother aided him. The children took it up, so that the wood surrounding us was filled with the hard high wail they made.

At last I was alone, myself and my little black ass. Off he went at a gallop until we left the wood behind us. I thought I had made a great bargain; where would one find an ass as lively and as spirited as my little black ass?

But when the wood was behind us, it was a different story. Not a foot would he stir. I thought I might tempt or coax him with soft words. He paid no heed to me. I tried shifting him with the stick. He wouldn't move an inch, he just stood there in the dead centre of the road.

People passed us by, some of them from the fair, and merry enough they were, too. I was advised to do this with him; I was advised to do that with him – but when one of them recommended that I carry him part of the way, I lost my patience and threw a shower of stones in the fellow's wake.

Finally I had to get down and – yes, drag him along behind me against the inclination of his legs....

You can see that I prayed devoutly for the travelling man who had sold me such a beast!

But it wasn't long before I noticed something odd. He was timid, and nothing frightened him as much as the music the wind makes in the branches of the trees.

As soon as he'd go under the boughs of the trees by the

road-side, he'd lose his sluggishness and could hardly be held in rein. First, he'd cock a listening ear; then he'd shake himself like a dog which had come out of the water; and before you'd know where you were, he'd be off at top speed. Right, said I.

I tied him to a gate. Off I went into the wood. I pulled an armful of fresh foliage. I made a wreath of it and put it around his neck and over his two ears as we were leaving the wood.

The poor beast! You never saw anything like the speed he made. From the music in his ears he imagined that he was still in the wood.

When we reached Ballyvaughan all the townspeople came out to see the wonder – myself and my little black ass decked with his crown of leafy branches....

I have the little black ass yet and will have till he dies. We have travelled many a long mile together in rain and drizzle, frost and snow. He lost some of his bad habits in the course of time – something I failed to do myself. And I think my little black ass knows that as well as anyone.

But he is as proud as punch since I bought him a lovely little bright-green cart. It's younger he's getting, poor beast!

Eileen O'Faoláin (1902-   )
Eileen O'Faoláin is a distinguished member of an extraordinary family.
Her husband, Seán, also contributes to this book; her daughter, Julia, is
a successful novelist and short-story writer.
'Cliona, Fairy Queen of Muskerry' is taken from one of her best-loved
children's books, *The Little Black Hen.*

Cliona, Fairy Queen of Muskerry

Eileen O'Faoláin

'WELL,' SAID BIDDY, 'no one could tell you better than I can,
for I know too much about her for my own good. She
scalded the heart in me and gave me no peace until I did her
bidding.'

As Biddy was talking she was glancing back over her
shoulder, out through the window. She spoke in a low tone,
almost in a whisper, as if she were afraid that someone
outside might hear her. Cossey Dearg too was uneasy on
her perch. Now and again she would ruffle her feathers and
cluck, cluck away to herself, as if she did not like what Biddy
was saying.

'What did she do to you at all?' said Garret.

'Every torment she could think of. And 'twas that old fairy
fort below there in the inch field that was the cause of it all.
Did you ever go in there after birds' nests, Garret?' said she,
knowing that he was very fond of bird-nesting.

'No,' said Garret. 'I'd be in dread of the good people who
live in it.'

'So well you might,' said she, 'for they do not like mortals
to be interfering with their places at all. Well, when you
cross over the briars that are growing around the mound in
the centre, there is a great big hole down in the middle of
the mound. In the bottom of that hole there is a pool of
water, and they say that if anyone fell into that pool, he'd go

124

down and down into Fairyland. There is an enchanted castle at the bottom, and when you reached there, you'd be put to work for them, and never again allowed back to earth.

'The fairy mist that sets people astray comes out of that hollow, and 'tis many a time I've seen it myself, and I standing there at the door of an evening. Out it comes like steam out of a kettle, and it rolls away up the hills. When I see it I always come in and close the door behind me, for 'tisn't right for anyone to see it or to be out in it.'

'Is it there Cliona lives?' said Julie.

'No, child, for she has a grand castle of her own inside the fairy doorway in the mountain, but she comes there to dance with her court on May Eves and Midsummer Nights. You can see plainly the fairy ring they have made with their dancing on top of the grassy mound.

'But to make a long story short, a few years ago, when I kept a few cows, one of them was a stray-away, and I was in mortal dread that he would go into the swamp in the fairy fort. And for that again I was not easy in my mind for them to be eating the grass on the fairy mound. "Maybe," said I to myself one day, "'tis bewitched I'll be after drinking their milk if they go in there to graze." So what did I do but get a man I had in the yard to put a fence of barbed wire around it, to keep the cows from going there.'

'And didn't Cliona like that?' said Garret.

'Like it, *astore*? I never knew what Cliona could do till then. First of all one cow died on me, and her calf after her. Another one, the stray-away, was ailing, and not a bit of butter could I churn. Then I was left without milk, for they used to milk the cows at night on me. And last of all didn't they dry up the well, and so I had not a drop of well water.

That went on till one day I said to myself I was no match for Cliona, and I told the man to take the fence away. After that I had no more trouble with her. The gadding cow got better, and I got a good price for her at the fair of Bantry. The well rose again, and I could make the bit of butter as always.'

'I suppose,' said Julie, 'she did not like the fort to be fenced in.'

'They couldn't drive up to the fort in their carriages when they'd be having a dance,' said Garret.

'That's it surely,' said Biddy. 'Anyway, once I took the fence away, she never troubled me again.'

'I wonder,' said Garret, 'what would happen if you tried to plough a fairy fort?'

'The Lord between us and all harm,' said Biddy, 'but 'twould be a queer person would think of the like, for everyone knows it isn't lucky. When I was a child, I often heard tell of a man over there beyond the hills, who tried to plough up one, and his two horses turned and attacked him. Another man who was ploughing in a field near-by had to come and whip them back from him.'

'My father told me,' said Julie, 'that there are crocks of gold hidden in the fort by the fairies, and if you could catch a leprechaun he'd tell you where they were.'

'That's true too,' said Biddy. 'I knew a man who got a pot of it, but he had no luck at all with it; his money melted like the froth of the river. The good people are best left alone, and that's why I am so worried about Cossey Dearg. I'm afraid Cliona will never rest until she gets her back into her clutches.'

Biddy and the three children fell silent. There was no chance of saving Cossey Dearg from such a one as Cliona. They looked into the fire. The kettle was singing on its hook, and the fire was burning brightly with leaping flames, throwing great big shadows up on the walls. On her perch sat the poor little sad hen, opening and shutting her eyes and looking as if she had no heart left for anything.

Garret made a sign to Julie to come outside. She knew then that he had something important to say to her – surely a plan to save Cossey Dearg. So they both said good-night to Biddy, and pushing back their stools they made out into the starlight and home down the *boreen*.

126

John O'Connor (1920-1960)
John O'Connor was born in County Armagh and started publishing
short stories when he was still a teenager. All of his work – including his
only novel, *Come Day–Go Day* – is a thinly disguised autobiographical
account of Neilly and his brothers growing up on the outskirts of his
native Armagh. He worked as a postman in Armagh before he emigrated
to Australia where he died in 1960. *Come Day–Go Day* has been reprinted
recently by The Blackstaff Press.

Neilly and the Fir Tree
John O'Connor

NEILLY WATCHED DREAMILY as the boy in the red jersey
dropped from the big fir-tree back on to the ground again.
The rest of the boys gathered round, calling out questions,
but Neilly didn't move. He stood with his hands behind his
back, a look of sadness in his large hazel eyes.

The boy in the red jersey shook his head, obviously very
thankful to be back on firm ground again.

'It's no good! Nobody'll ever be able to climb that tree.'

He was the third to have attempted it. Two of the others
had already tried, but they also had failed. The boy in the
red jersey had the name of being the best climber of them
all, and now that the big fir had beaten him too, well it
didn't seem much good for anyone else to try.

He shook his head again. 'Nobody'll ever be able to climb
that tree.... You might be able to get *past* that part all right,
but you'd never be able to get down again. You'd be stuck
up there all night. Isn't that right, Franky?'

All the boys walked backwards out into the field, staring
upwards, until halfway up the tree, they could see the bare
part like a faint magic girdle encircling the trunk. Here for a
space of about six or seven feet the trunk was devoid of
branches. The boys argued and shook their heads. No one
took the slightest notice of little Neilly standing a few yards
away.

127

There were three firs here on top of the hill. Like three monuments erected by some long-vanished race of giants, they towered up into the air, a landmark for miles around.

Neilly gave a faint shudder as he looked up into the fir. He felt so terribly small and insignificant beside this glowering monster. Neilly was a small slight lad of about nine. He was easily the youngest and smallest of the entire group. His legs and arms were slender as reeds, and he wore a pair of ponderous-looking black boots – no stockings. His right boot was soaking wet, and smeared with pale, gluey mud. That was where he had nearly fallen into St Bridget's drain, about ten minutes ago. Everyone else had jumped it except him. Poor Neilly! How he wished he were a bit bigger, so that he could jump and climb as well as the other lads. It wasn't his fault that he was so small, but the rest of the boys didn't think of that. When they did anything that he couldn't, they just jeered at him, or worse even – ignored him altogether. Neilly suddenly became aware of his companions' glances.

The boy in the red jersey was pointing at him dramatically.

'There you are!' he shouted. 'I bet you Neilly could climb it though. Couldn't you, Neilly?'

'Ah, he can't even jump St Bridget's drain, yet, even,' another boy chimed in. At this Neilly bit his lip, hiding his wet, muddy boot behind his dry left one.

The boys came closer.

'Ah, poor wee Neilly! What are you blushing about, Neilly? What are you blushing about?'

The boy in the red jersey stuck his hands up.

'I still say that Neilly could climb that tree.' He put his hand on Neilly's shoulder. 'Couldn't you, Neilly?'

Neilly shook the hand off instantly. The boy gave him a push, and then the rest of the boys began pushing him too. Neilly became infuriated. He made a wild swing with his boot, but the boys only jeered louder. Neilly's rage increased. He broke through his tormentors, and rushed over to the fir.

'For two pins I would climb your ould tree for you,' he raged. 'D'you think I couldn't, like?'

The jeering grew louder. The boys were enjoying themselves immensely. With a mighty effort Neilly forced himself to be calm. He turned to the tree. The lower part of the enormous trunk was worn smooth and shiny, where the cows had come to scratch. Neilly stripped off his boots. Then, standing on a great, hump-backed root, he gave a jump, reaching for a huge, rusty staple which was driven into the trunk about five feet off the ground. He caught it, skinning his knee against the bark. He made another lunge towards the first branch a little higher, and drew himself up, casting a swift, triumphant glance at the boys below.

As he climbed he became filled with joy. The rich spicy scent of resin hung in the air like incense, and his hands and feet grew rough and sticky, which, of course, made his progress all the more easy.

Now and then he glanced through the heavy, green foliage. The fields seemed a great distance below, but the thrill he felt was one of daring rather than of fear. He could hear the faint sound of his name being called by the boys below. But he urged on, too excited to answer.

He came at last to the bare part, and here, craning up, he caught his breath in dismay. Except for a few withered branches, the column of the tree was bare indeed. Above, near enough to mock him, but far enough to frighten him, the heavy growth of the tree was resumed. In some past storm perhaps, a sabre of lightning had put its brand here, killing the branches but leaving the bole itself unharmed.

With a sinking heart Neilly circled the tree, searching for a reliable grip, but there was nothing except those few, puny branches, and they looked too frail to bear even his weight.

It would be terrible to have to turn back now. For a moment he felt like risking all in one mad hopeless leap for the foliage above. Then a look of fierce determination settled on his face.

One of the stricken branches grew just within reach of his fingers. He gripped it cautiously as near to the trunk as possible. He pressed gingerly and it gave a few ominous creaks. The pounding of his heart increased. Gradually he pulled at the branch until at last his entire weight was drooping from it. Hardly daring to breathe, he prised himself up inch by inch, and then grabbed frantically at another branch higher up. He closed his eyes fully expecting it to snap, but although it gave a loud, terrifying creak and shivered alarmingly, it held. Panting, he struggled up until he was able to stand on the bottom branch.

For a minute he hugged the trunk afraid to move another inch. The rough, scenty bole of the fir, seemed the most beautiful thing in the world. Then, fearfully, he allowed his eyes to creep upwards. Tremblingly, he reached up with his right hand, scraping it over the bark, but six inches separated his fingers from the lowermost living branch. He glanced down at the rotten branch he was standing on, and his head began to spin. For a time he stood pressed against the trunk, groaning softly to himself.

Then he looked up and reached his hand out again. He eased himself gently away from the trunk, keeping his eyes fixed as though by hypnotism on the branch above. The tip of his tongue stuck out. His legs bent slightly. Then he *sprang*.

With a loud crack, the branch below him broke off, but at the same time the fingers of his right hand closed over the one above, and he hung, swinging wildly. He brought his left hand up, gave himself a few twisting heaves, and then he was sitting safely on the branch, panting like an exhausted runner.

He got up at last and climbed on up the trunk that was tapering now. He climbed fast and impatiently as though he were being pursued by someone, and at last he came to the very top.

He stood spell-bound, with the tiny green world stretched beneath, like a view from a picture book. The cows and the sheep in the far off fields looked like tiny plasticine toys. A small cold breeze probed through his jersey making him shiver and the tree swayed gently, sending a quaint thrill through his stomach. Below him, down the great spine of the fir, the pale brown branches jutted out like a framework of bones.

Neilly shouted, calling the names of the boys below, and soon he saw them, running like little gnomes over the field, and down the hill. He had to laugh at them. He could hear their thin excited chatter, as they pointed upwards, shading their eyes. Neilly hung there enraptured. His heart swelled

131

and the keen fresh air stung the inside of his nostrils, making his eyes swim. Then at last he gave the boys one last wave and started down again. The boys still stood below pointing upwards engrossed in his descent.

When he reached the bare part again, he sat on a branch and swung his legs. He felt very calm, as though he were only stopping for a rest. Then gradually he became uneasy. He stood up, rubbing his wrist over his lips, and glancing this way and that. Far far below, so far that he now shuddered, he could see the boys still hunched together, pointing. He could hear their shouts, tiny pin points of sound. 'Ah he's stuck now. He'll never get down now....'

Neilly circled the tree, searching for a toe hold, but the only one had vanished when that dead branch had snapped beneath him. Hardly knowing what he was doing, he swung out on a branch and hung down weaving to and fro. He looked down along his chest beyond his twisting legs, feasting his eyes on the branches below. His feet clawed out, trying to grasp at them. Suddenly there was a crack and the branch broke! He gave a terrified cry, and his body dropped like a plummet.

With a shock that jarred his whole body, both his feet struck a branch directly underneath. He sagged forward, but at the same moment, his out-thrust hands closed over another branch above him, blocking his headlong fall. He hung for a moment, stretched between the two branches, in a kind of daze.

Then in a little while he recovered, and began to clamber on down. Once he missed his foothold, and almost fell again. He felt a streak of pain along the inside of his leg, above the knee, as a ragged twig tore the skin. But he continued on his way.

Gradually his strength returned, and when he at last dropped back on to solid earth, he was smiling, and his eyes shone. The instant he hit the ground again, the boys swarmed around, cheering and clapping him on the back. Neilly retreated a few steps, breathlessly.

'Good man, Neilly!' the boy in the red jersey was shouting. 'You did what nobody else here the day would have done. Boy-oh-boy when we seen you dropping down that bare part there, we sure thought you were a goner.

Didn't we boys?'

'We sure did!' the rest of the boys chorused. 'That was powerful, Neilly.'

'Dropping down?' Neilly thought. 'Dropping down?' He opened his mouth to say, 'but the branch broke. I didn't drop. I fell!'

Then he stopped. If they thought he had dropped it, well, let them. He *would* have dropped it anyway, if the branch he was standing on hadn't broken off first and foremost. Of course he would! He would have dropped it like anything!

Anyway, fall, or drop, he had climbed the tree, and that's what nobody else had done. Ha, he'd shown them, so he had! They wouldn't jeer at him now! It wouldn't be 'poor wee Neilly' any more now....

The boys brought his boots over for him, and the boy in the red jersey cleaned his muddy one with grass.

As Neilly was sitting down putting on his boots, his trousers slipped up, and he was surprised to see a long red scratch on his leg. Then he remembered where he had slipped on his downward journey.

The boys all bent down to examine the wound, and they began advising him to come home, and get some iodine on it. Neilly smiled. It was only a scratch really, and not painful at all, but for some reason he felt terribly proud of it.

As the boys escorted him over the fields, home, he put on a slight limp, and every twenty yards or so, he would glance back at the middle fir that he'd climbed, and then down at his leg again, and then back to the fir again, and his eyes were shining with wonder, and joy.

133

Micheál mac Liammóir (1899-1978)
Micheál mac Liammóir was born in Cork in 1899. *Faery Nights*, the book
from which this story was taken, was written and illustrated by him
before he was twenty, and his versions of the stories appeared in English
and Irish on facing pages. In 1928 he founded with his English partner,
Hilton Edwards, the Gate Theatre in Dublin. He became a world-famous
actor and still found time to write plays, stories, and an autobiographical
novel.

St. Brigid's Eve

Micheál mac Liammóir

HER NAME WAS GRÁINNE, but she wasn't at all like the princess
in the old tale. This Gráinne was a little girl with a snub
nose, black hair, and shiny grey eyes. Gráinne lived in
Dublin; she had so many dolls that she couldn't count them,
a little black dog which she called Bedelia, and any amount
of pretty dresses. Gráinne was spoilt.

She lived in Dublin, as I said before. Indeed, her house
was right in the middle of the city. But if you had asked her
did she like the same city, she would have said that she
'preferred the country'. She often used to pay visits to the
country, too: she used to stay with her Aunt Lily, who had a
nice house in County Limerick. Aunt Lily took a great
interest in old Irish things, and wore queer dresses of blue
and green; she was very learned, too, and wore spectacles,
and she used to say to Gráinne:

'Why don't you give the little dog a nice Irish name, child
– Sceolán, or Bran, or Sciarlóg, for example?'

'No, I prefer Bedelia.'

Gráinne was very spoilt.

She was rather naughty, too. For instance, when she
stayed in the country with her aunt, she used always to be
roaming about all over the place, in spite of all her poor aunt
could say, with no company but Bedelia. And as Aunt Lily
said, Bedelia was no good at all for protection. She was a

silly little black dog, with a fluffy tail, which could do nothing but yelp. But Gráinne gave her the love of her heart, and would never move a step without Bedelia.

And so it happened that Bedelia played an important part in the adventure which befell Gráinne one Saint Brigid's Eve, when she was staying with her aunt. Aunt Lily had planned to hold the feast in the proper way when night came, and she was very busy during the day making cakes and things for it.

'To-night, my dear,' said she to Gráinne, 'we'll have great fun, as it's Saint Brigid's Eve. We'll have a grand feast, and light the candles in the correct manner, and I'll invite those nice little Sullivans to come in and play with you....'

'Yes, auntie,' said Gráinne meekly, but she said to herself: 'There! How I hate those stupid little Sullivans! I always want to play Blind-Man's-Buff, and they can do nothing at all but play marbles, or 'Four Corners', or something of the sort.... But I know! I'll go out for a walk, and maybe when I come in they'll be gone.'

And so when darkness fell, and her aunt began lighting some long white candles she had arranged in the window, Gráinne took little Bedelia in her arms and stole out of the house, and off she went over the fields. It was rather cold, and Gráinne only had on a blue cotton dress with black dots speckled on it – she had forgotten to put on her coat – but she ran quickly, and soon she was quite warm. She had a grand time. Once she fell into a ditch while she was looking for primroses (she didn't find one), and when she climbed out again her dress was smeared with mud, and her feet were wet; and another time what should Bedelia do but fall in a pool – and she was not able to swim – and Gráinne herself nearly fell in, too, trying to rescue her darling. She caught hold of her at last, however, and they both went gaily on.

Before long they discovered a little stream which Gráinne had never seen before. She thought it would be great sport to follow it. So off she set, with Bedelia running by her side, sniffing round and pretending that she was looking for water rats; though it's likely if one had come out she would have been terrified.

It was a lovely little stream. It made a queer gurgling noise

135

as it ran over the stones.

'I wonder where did it come from?' said Gráinne to herself, as she wandered along, following the tip of her nose. She didn't notice that the little white stars were coming out in the sky, or that the sun was sinking behind the hills, or that there was a cold edge on the wind. It seemed to her that the sound the stream made was very like the music of a flute she had heard played by some man in Dublin once. Indeed, you would think it was the music of a flute, and not a stream at all. Gráinne stood still for a second, listening intently. Bedelia pricked up her ears too and, if you would believe it, she didn't bark once for five whole minutes. After a while they went on.

The stream ran here and there at its own sweet will, among stones and rocks and over smooth green grass. Gráinne was a long way from home by now. But she didn't think of that. She just followed the stream, and wondered at the music it was making. Presently it turned a corner, round a big grey rock. She followed it, climbing over the rock with great care, so as not to wet her feet again. Bedelia ran along with her feet in the water, which was filling by this time with the reflections of twinkling stars, and she kept very quiet. They were round the corner by now; and the music of the stream was even louder than before. Gráinne lifted her head, and what should she see in front of her but – a wood.

It was a wood of tall bare trees, very dark and lovely-looking. The branches were stirring and sighing in the wind. How black and shadowy it looked in among the trees! You would be frightened to go into their midst unless you were very brave, indeed, and had a good bright lantern. And Gráinne was not one of the bravest little girls in Ireland.... She started. She didn't know why, but she started. She gave a little whistle, and then she began talking to Bedelia.

'What a funny wood!' said she, but then she stopped. Bedelia had vanished from her side and was making straight for the wood, with her nose to the ground.

'I'll follow her,' said Gráinne, and off she ran after the dog, calling:
'Bedelia! Bedelia!'
Her voice sounded strange and empty in the deep

stillness, and she stopped. For everything was extraordinarily quiet, but for the sighing of the wind among the trees. There was no music from the stream! Gráinne noticed this suddenly. She ran on, but she didn't call out again. And before long, what should she see but her own darling Bedelia standing by a tree at the edge of the wood.

Bedelia was trembling. Her eyes were as big as two pennies, and her fur was bristling.

'What's the matter?' said Gráinne, but as she spoke the sweet reedy music began to play again. Over she went to Bedelia, and she gave a peep in through the trees.

'Oh!' said she.

A little green man, with a red cap on his head, was sitting under a tree, playing a pipe. It was quite plain that he was a faery man – or why would he be wearing a red cap? And who, but one of the Good People, could make such sweet music? Gráinne was delighted to see a faery, and before long she noticed that there were three others there – tiny, funny little men – sitting on toadstools, listening to the music.

Now, Gráinne had heard once that if you could catch a faery you'd be able to make him tell you where to find a crock of gold, or maybe a bag of precious stones. Wouldn't that be grand! She would have loved to find such a priceless treasure, and to show it to her aunt. And wouldn't she be surprised, and everyone else too! The whole world would think what a wonderful child she was....

'Gráinne Burke?' people would say. 'Oh, yes, that wonderful little girl who found the crock of gold. Such a clever little darling!'

Gráinne forgot that the wood was so dark and gloomy. She forgot that she didn't know her way in it, and that the night was falling fast. She sprang out from behind the tree.

'Come on, Bedelia,' she cried, and she jumped over the stream to where the faery men were sitting. But if she did, they were too quick for her.

'A child! A child! A human child!' they screamed, and away they rushed, with Gráinne and Bedelia close behind them.

What a chase it was! Gráinne was soon out of breath, but she wouldn't give in. She meant to get that crock of gold somehow. She stumbled over stones and she fell over roots, but she didn't succeed in catching the faeries. And presently she gave a shout of anger.

'Bad cess to you!' she cried tearfully, and she sat down on the ground. 'You're gone now,' said she, 'and I didn't find any gold at all.'

And she laid her head on her hands and started to cry. But soon she looked up. She brushed the tears from her cheeks. What on earth was Bedelia doing? She was scraping and scratching the old withered leaves that covered the ground, directly in the spot where she had seen the faery people vanishing from her sight. Her black fluffy tail was wagging, and it was plain that she was very excited.

'What is it now at all?' said Gráinne crossly.

But Bedelia went on scratching and scraping. Gráinne looked at her in surprise. But what was that? The gleam of something bright. She rose to her feet and went over to where the little dog was working so hard. She knelt down, stooping low so as to see what it was....

'A necklace!' said she, and she held it up. 'An old necklace! Oh! – and I thought it would be a crock of gold.... And it's not shiny a bit except here and there, and it's covered with earth.... Well, I don't care – it'll do for a collar for you, darling!' And she fastened it round Bedelia's neck.

Now I ought to tell you here that Bedelia had never worn a collar in her life, and I suppose she was too old to start practising new ways. At any rate, she didn't like it at all, and look! she started rushing round and round like the wheel of an old cart going down a steep hill. She bit her tail, she threw her four feet into the air, she gave the most awful barks, and suddenly – off she flew like an arrow you'd shoot out of a bow.

Poor Gráinne! What could she do? She was already too tired to run any more, she thought, but wouldn't anything be better for her than to be left all night in the gloomy, murmuring wood? And nobody to talk to but the ghosts of the trees and the spirits of the woods. So up she jumped and fled away through the wood after the dog. It was darker than ever now, and I daresay you will be asking me how could she see Bedelia at all, for Bedelia was blacker even than the wood. And but for a queer light that was shining

139

from the necklace round Bedelia's neck, she would not have seen her, or her shadow. But that was what saved her, that gleaming golden light which rushed through the trees like a thread of fire. She followed this beautiful sign straight on, and after a long while they were out of the wood. It was really night by this time, and there was neither star nor moon in the sky and, to make the story seven times worse, it was raining heavily – splash, splash, splash!

Poor Gráinne was terribly tired; she had no breath left; she was drowned by the rain and smeared with the soft mud of the roads and fields; and she was certain that all the faeries in Ireland were after her, and after Bedelia too, because they had stolen the old necklace. But at last, and long last, just as she was saying to herself that she couldn't go a step further, she saw a big dark house in front of her, with bright lights glinting through the windows, and she recognized her aunt's home. She ran in through the gate, across the garden, still following Bedelia, and a moment later she was in Aunt Lily's arms, and Aunt Lily was kissing her fondly and saying:

'Gráinne, you bold child, where were you, or why did you run off like that – and I thought I'd never see you again!'

And she was so pleased that she gave her a little slap on the ear.

'And the Sullivans came and ate up every cake there was, and they went home ages ago, and – oh, but we must get these wet clothes off immediately, my pet, and get a glass of hot lemonade or something –'

(Aunt Lily was terrified of colds, you see, and things of the sort.)

'And oh, Gráinne!' said she, 'how could you leave me like that?' And she kissed her again.

And it wasn't long before Gráinne was sitting up in her own little bed, drinking bread and milk, and telling her auntie all about her adventures. During the talk, however, Bedelia jumped up on to the bed, and began to dance and leap up and down, just as she had done an hour or so before that in the gloomy wood.

'Is she mad, or what's the matter with her at all?' cried Aunt Lily. She had never liked Bedelia – on account of her

Englishy name, maybe. 'Is she mad?' said she.

'No, auntie,' said Gráinne. 'It's the necklace, I think.'

'The necklace?'

'Yes. I didn't come to that part of the story yet –'

And she was just going to begin, when Aunt Lily gave a little scream. She caught hold of Bedelia – a thing she had never done before.

'But what's this?' said she, and there was a tremble in her voice.

She unfastened the necklace from Bedelia's neck. She went over to the lamp and examined it closely. A flush came into her old face. She took off her spectacles and rubbed them, and then she settled them on the top of her nose again. She bent down over the necklace....

Gráinne grew tired watching her. She couldn't help closing her eyes, and pretty soon her head sank back on the soft white pillow. But before she fell asleep she heard her aunt talking softly to herself.

'An old Irish necklace,' she was saying. 'An old, old Irish necklace! The most beautiful one I have ever seen.... And it's pure red gold. And to think – I hardly believed her when she was talking about the little green man – and yet they say that it's true that they are still here, that they know where gold is to be found. I wonder...'

Frank O'Connor (1903-1966)
Frank O'Connor's real name was Michael O'Donovan. He was born in
Cork in 1903 and he wrote plays, novels, biography and autobiography,
but his best work is his short stories and translations from old Irish
poetry. He wrote several stories about his own childhood in Cork. In
these, childhood is not like something remembered from years before,
but more like something that is actually happening. The art of the best of
these stories is that we believe we hear the young boy speaking.

First Confession
Frank O'Connor

ALL THE TROUBLE BEGAN when my grandfather died and my
grandmother – my father's mother – came to live with us.
Relations in the one house are a strain at the best of times,
but, to make matters worse, my grandmother was a real old
countrywoman and quite unsuited to the life in town. She
had a fat, wrinkled old face, and, to Mother's great
indignation, went round the house in bare feet – the boots
had her crippled, she said. For dinner she had a jug of
porter and a pot of potatoes with – sometimes – a bit of salt
fish, and she poured out the potatoes on the table and ate
them slowly, with great relish, using her fingers by way of a
fork.

Now, girls are supposed to be fastidious, but I was the
one who suffered most from this. Nora, my sister, just
sucked up to the old woman for the penny she got every
Friday out of the old-age pension, a thing I could not do. I
was too honest, that was my trouble; and when I was
playing with Bill Connell, the sergeant-major's son, and saw
my grandmother steering up the path with the jug of porter
sticking out from beneath her shawl I was mortified. I made
excuses not to let him come into the house, because I could
never be sure what she would be up to when we went in.

When Mother was at work and my grandmother made the
dinner I wouldn't touch it. Nora once tried to make me, but

I hid under the table from her and took the bread-knife with me for protection. Nora let on to be very indignant (she wasn't, of course, but she knew Mother saw through her, so she sided with Gran) and came after me. I lashed out at her with the bread-knife, and after that she left me alone. I stayed there till Mother came in from work and made my dinner, but when Father came in later Nora said in a shocked voice: 'Oh, Dadda, do you know what Jackie did at dinnertime?' Then, of course, it all came out; Father gave me a flaking; Mother interfered, and for days after that he didn't speak to me and Mother barely spoke to Nora. And all because of that old woman! God knows, I was heart-scalded.

Then, to crown my misfortunes, I had to make my first confession and communion. It was an old woman called Ryan who prepared us for these. She was about the one age with Gran; she was well-to-do, lived in a big house on Montenotte, wore a black cloak and bonnet, and came every day to school at three o'clock when we should have been going home, and talked to us of hell. She may have mentioned the other place as well, but that could only have been by accident, for hell had the first place in her heart.

She lit a candle, took out a new half-crown, and offered it to the first boy who would hold one finger – only one finger! – in the flame for five minutes by the school clock. Being always very ambitious I was tempted to volunteer, but I thought it might look greedy. Then she asked were we afraid of holding one finger – only one finger! – in a little candle flame for five minutes and not afraid of burning all over in roasting hot furnaces for all eternity. 'All eternity! Just think of that! A whole lifetime goes by and it's nothing, not even a drop in the ocean of your sufferings.' The woman was really interesting about hell, but my attention was all fixed on the half-crown. At the end of the lesson she put it back in her purse. It was a great disappointment; a religious woman like that, you wouldn't think she'd bother about a thing like a half-crown.

Another day she said she knew a priest who woke one night to find a fellow he didn't recognize leaning over the end of his bed. The priest was a bit frightened – naturally enough – but he asked the fellow what he wanted, and the fellow said in a deep, husky voice that he wanted to go to confession. The priest said it was an awkward time and wouldn't it do in the morning, but the fellow said that last time he went to confession, there was one sin he kept back, being ashamed to mention it, and now it was always on his mind. Then the priest knew it was a bad case, because the fellow was after making a bad confession and committing a mortal sin. He got up to dress, and just then the cock crew in the yard outside, and – lo and behold! – when the priest looked round there was no sign of the fellow, only a smell of burning timber, and when the priest looked at his bed didn't he see the print of two hands burned in it? That was because the fellow had made a bad confession. This story made a shocking impression on me.

But the worst of all was when she showed us how to examine our conscience. Did we take the name of the Lord, our God, in vain? Did we honour our father and our mother? (I asked her did this include grandmothers and she said it did.) Did we love our neighbours as ourselves? Did we covet our neighbour's goods? (I thought of the way I felt about the penny that Nora got every Friday.) I decided that between one thing and another, I must have broken the whole ten commandments, all on account of that old woman, and so far as I could see, so long as she remained in the house I had no hope of ever doing anything else.

I was scared to death of confession. The day the whole class went I let on to have a toothache, hoping my absence wouldn't be noticed; but at three o'clock, just as I was feeling safe, along comes a chap with a message from Mrs. Ryan that I was to go to confession myself on Saturday and be at the chapel for communion with the rest. To make it worse, Mother couldn't come with me and sent Nora instead.

Now, that girl had ways of tormenting me that Mother never knew of. She held my hand as we went down the hill, smiling sadly and saying how sorry she was for me, as if she were bringing me to the hospital for an operation.

'Oh, God help us!' she moaned. 'Isn't it a terrible pity you weren't a good boy? Oh, Jackie, my heart bleeds for you! How will you ever think of all your sins? Don't forget you have to tell him about the time you kicked Gran on the shin.'

'Lemme go!' I said, trying to drag myself free of her. 'I don't want to go to confession at all.'

'But sure, you'll have to go to confession, Jackie,' she replied in the same regretful tone. 'Sure, if you didn't, the parish priest would be up to the house, looking for you. 'Tisn't, God knows, that I'm not sorry for you. Do you remember the time you tried to kill me with the bread-knife under the table? And the language you used to me? I don't know what he'll do with you at all, Jackie. He might have to send you up to the bishop.'

I remember thinking bitterly that she didn't know the half of what I had to tell – if I told it. I knew I couldn't tell it, and understood perfectly why the fellow in Mrs. Ryan's story made a bad confession; it seemed to me a great shame that people wouldn't stop criticizing him. I remember that steep hill down to the church, and the sunlit hillsides beyond the valley of the river, which I saw in the gaps between the houses like Adam's last glimpse of Paradise.

Then, when she had manoeuvred me down the long flight of steps to the chapel yard, Nora suddenly changed her tone. She became the raging malicious devil she really was.

'There you are!' she said with a yelp of triumph, hurling me through the church door. 'And I hope he'll give you the penitential psalms, you dirty little caffler.'

I knew then I was lost, given up to eternal justice. The door with the coloured-glass panels swung shut behind me, the sunlight went out and gave place to deep shadow, and the wind whistled outside so that the silence within seemed to crackle like ice under my feet. Nora sat in front of me by the confession box. There were a couple of old women ahead of her, and then a miserable-looking poor devil came and wedged me in at the other side, so that I couldn't escape even if I had the courage. He joined his hands and rolled his eyes in the direction of the roof, muttering aspirations in an anguished tone, and I wondered had he a grandmother too. Only a grandmother could account for a fellow behaving in that heartbroken way, but he was better off than I, for he at least could go and confess his sins; while I would make a bad confession and then die in the night and be continually coming back and burning people's furniture.

Nora's turn came, and I heard the sound of something slamming, and then her voice as if butter wouldn't melt in her mouth, and then another slam, and out she came. God, the hypocrisy of women! Her eyes were lowered, her head was bowed, and her hands were joined very low down on her stomach, and she walked up the aisle to the side altar looking like a saint. You never saw such an exhibition of devotion; and I remembered the devilish malice with which she had tormented me all the way from our door, and wondered were all religious people like that, really. It was my turn now. With the fear of damnation in my soul I went in, and the confessional door closed of itself behind me.

It was pitch-dark and I couldn't see priest or anything else. Then I really began to be frightened. In the darkness it was a matter between God and me, and He had all the odds. He knew what my intentions were before I even started; I had no chance. All I had ever been told about confession got mixed up in my mind, and I knelt to one wall and said: 'Bless me, father, for I have sinned; this is my first confession.' I waited for a few minutes, but nothing happened, so I tried it on the other wall. Nothing happened there either. He had me spotted all right.

It must have been then that I noticed the shelf at about one height with my head. It was really a place for grown-up people to rest their elbows, but in my distracted state I thought it was probably the place you were supposed to kneel. Of course, it was on the high side and not very deep, but I was always good at climbing and managed to get up all right. Staying up was the trouble. There was room only for my knees, and nothing you could get a grip on but a sort of wooden moulding a bit above it. I held on to the moulding and repeated the words a little louder, and this time something happened all right. A slide was slammed back; a little light entered the box, and a man's voice said: 'Who's there?'

''Tis me, father,' I said for fear he mightn't see me and go away again. I couldn't see him at all. The place the voice came from was under the moulding, about level with my knees, so I took a good grip of the moulding and swung myself down till I saw the astonished face of a young priest looking up at me. He had to put his head on one side to see

146

me, and I had to put mine on one side to see him, so we were more or less talking to one another upside-down. It struck me as a queer way of hearing confessions, but I didn't feel it my place to criticize.

'Bless me, father, for I have sinned; this is my first confession,' I rattled off all in one breath, and swung myself down the least shade more to make it easier for him.

'What are you doing up there?' he shouted in an angry voice, and the strain the politeness was putting on my hold of the moulding, and the shock of being addressed in such an uncivil tone, were too much for me. I lost my grip, tumbled, and hit the door an unmerciful wallop before I found myself flat on my back in the middle of the aisle. The people who had been waiting stood up with their mouths open. The priest opened the door of the middle box and came out, pushing his biretta back from his forehead; he looked something terrible. Then Nora came scampering down the aisle.

'Oh, you dirty little caffler!' she said. 'I might have known you'd do it. I might have known you'd disgrace me. I can't leave you out of my sight for one minute.'

Before I could even get to my feet to defend myself she bent down and gave me a clip across the ear. This reminded me that I was so stunned I had even forgotten to cry, so that people might think I wasn't hurt at all, when in fact I was probably maimed for life. I gave a roar out of me.

'What's all this about?' the priest hissed, getting angrier than ever and pushing Nora off me. 'How dare you hit the child like that, you little vixen!'

'But I can't do my penance with him, father,' Nora cried, cocking an outraged eye up at him.

'Well, go and do it, or I'll give you some more to do,' he said, giving me a hand up. 'Was it coming to confession you were, my poor man?' he asked me.

''Twas, father,' said I with a sob.

'Oh,' he said respectfully, 'a big hefty fellow like you must have terrible sins. Is this your first?'

''Tis, father,' said I.

'Worse and worse,' he said gloomily. 'The crimes of a life-time. I don't know will I get rid of you at all today. You'd better wait now till I'm finished with these old ones. You

147

can see by the looks of them they haven't much to tell.'

'I will, father,' I said with something approaching joy.

The relief of it was really enormous. Nora stuck out her tongue at me from behind his back, but I couldn't even be bothered retorting. I knew from the very moment that man opened his mouth that he was intelligent above the ordinary. When I had time to think, I saw how right I was. It only stood to reason that a fellow confessing after seven years would have more to tell than people that went every week. The crimes of a lifetime, exactly as he said. It was only what he expected, and the rest was the cackle of old women and girls with their talk of hell, the bishop, and the penitential psalms. That was all they knew. I started to make my examination of conscience, and barring the one bad business of my grandmother it didn't seem so bad.

The next time, the priest steered me into the confession box himself and left the shutter back the way I could see him get in and sit down at the further side of the grille from me.

'Well, now,' he said, 'what do they call you?'

'Jackie, father,' said I.

'And what's a-trouble to you, Jackie?'

'Father,' I said, feeling I might as well get it over while I had him in good humour, 'I had it all arranged to kill my grandmother.'

He seemed a bit shaken by that, all right, because he said nothing for quite a while.

'My goodness,' he said at last, 'that'd be a shocking thing to do. What put that into your head?'

'Father,' I said, feeling very sorry for myself, 'she's an awful woman.'

'Is she?' he asked. 'What way is she awful?'

'She takes porter, father,' I said, knowing well from the way Mother talked of it that this was a mortal sin, and hoping it would make the priest take a more favourable view of my case.

'Oh, my!' he said, and I could see he was impressed.

'And snuff, father,' said I.

'That's a bad case, sure enough, Jackie,' he said.

'And she goes round in her bare feet, father,' I went on in a rush of self-pity, 'and she knows I don't like her, and she gives pennies to Nora and none to me, and my da sides with

148

her and flakes me, and one night I was so heart-scalded I made up my mind I'd have to kill her.'

'And what would you do with the body?' he asked with great interest.

'I was thinking I could chop that up and carry it away in a barrow I have,' I said.

'Begor, Jackie,' he said, 'do you know you're a terrible child?'

'I know, father,' I said, for I was just thinking the same thing myself. 'I tried to kill Nora too with a bread-knife under the table, only I missed her.'

'Is that the little girl that was beating you just now?' he asked.

''Tis, father.'

'Someone will go for her with a bread-knife one day, and he won't miss her,' he said rather cryptically. 'You must have great courage. Between ourselves, there's a lot of people I'd like to do the same to but I'd never have the nerve. Hanging is an awful death.'

'Is it, father?' I asked with the deepest interest – I was always very keen on hanging. 'Did you ever see a fellow hanged?'

'Dozens of them,' he said solemnly. 'And they all died roaring.'

'Jay!' I said.

'Oh, a horrible death!' he said with great satisfaction. 'Lots of the fellows I saw killed their grandmothers too, but they all said 'twas never worth it.'

He had me there for a full ten minutes talking, and then walked out the chapel yard with me. I was genuinely sorry to part with him, because he was the most entertaining character I'd ever met in the religious line. Outside, after the shadow of the church, the sunlight was like the roaring of waves on a beach; it dazzled me; and when the frozen silence melted and I heard the screech of trams on the road my heart soared. I knew now I wouldn't die in the night and come back, leaving marks on my mother's furniture. It would be a great worry to her, and the poor soul had enough.

Nora was sitting on the railing, waiting for me, and she put on a very sour puss when she saw the priest with me.

She was mad jealous because a priest had never come out of the church with her.

'Well,' she asked coldly, after he left me, 'what did he give you?'

'Three Hail Marys,' I said.

'Three Hail Marys,' she repeated incredulously. 'You mustn't have told him anything.'

'I told him everything,' I said confidently.

'About Gran and all?'

'About Gran and all.'

(All she wanted was to be able to go home and say I'd made a bad confession.)

'Did you tell him you went for me with the bread-knife?' she asked with a frown.

'I did to be sure.'

'And he only gave you three Hail Marys?'

'That's all.'

She slowly got down from the railing with a baffled air. Clearly, this was beyond her. As we mounted the steps back to the main road she looked at me suspiciously.

'What are you sucking?' she asked.

'Bullseyes.'

'Was it the priest gave them to you?'

''Twas.'

'Lord God,' she wailed bitterly, 'some people have all the luck! 'Tis no advantage to anybody trying to be good. I might just as well be a sinner like you.'

Maura Laverty (1907-1966)
This is probably a true story. The account of a little girl's happy
childhood in her grandmother's house in the village of Ballyderrig is
most likely an account of Maura Laverty's own childhood. She was born
and raised by her grandmother in a village in County Kildare before
going to Spain to work as a governess and later as a journalist.
Far from the cities and shops children had few possessions in those
days, and those that they had, they treasured. This extract tells of the
arrival of Delia's first bicycle. When *Never No More* was first published in
1942 Seán O'Faoláin in the introduction described his reaction to it as
'love at first sight'.

After Summer
Maura Laverty

An excerpt from *Never No More*

THE CONVENT SCHOOL REOPENED on the second Monday in
August. I was put into seventh class with Mary Joe
Heffernan and Bridie Murray of the bog. I had no great taste
for lessons, and it's little work I would have done if Sister
Mary Patrick who taught Fifth, Sixth, and Seventh, and who
knew that Grandmother wanted to make a teacher out of
me, had not kept a close eye on me.

Sometimes I was sent in to mind the Babies while their
teacher, Sister Mary Anthony, who was in charge of the
Convent garden, went to make sure that Paddy Moloney,
the gardener, was not idling or eating the pears.

I was green with envy when I reached school that first
morning after the holidays. Mary Joe Heffernan, whose
father was one of the biggest farmers around Ballyderrig,
and Bridie Murray, whose mother kept a public-house at
Brackna Crossroads, had each of them a new bike.

The two-mile walk home from the town was hard on me
that evening. The road to Derrymore had never seemed so
long, and I kept thinking of how short it would be if only I
had a bike. To make it even longer, a partridge flew down

152

on the road right in front of me just as I came abreast of Doran's wheat field. It seemed to have a broken wing or an injured leg, for, as I neared it, it fluttered lopsidedly across the road and through the hedge into the field. I followed the partridge through a gap in the hedge and was just in time to see it alight in the centre of the wheat. Well, there was no following it there, for like every country child I had respect for growing things, and if Maeterlinck's blue bird had alighted three yards from where I stood and I had recognized it for what it was, it would not have tempted me to tread on the ripening wheat.

I plucked an ear of the wheat and, as Grandmother had taught me to do, I blessed myself with it three times – once for the food it stood for, once for the prosperity it represented, and lastly because the Consecrated Host was made of wheat.

When I reached Derrymore House I was later than usual.

'You're late,' Gran said to me. 'What kept you?'

'Ah, it's a long old road, Gran,' I answered.

'That's the first time I heard you complain of it,' was her dry comment. 'Are your legs going on you?'

'If I'd a bike, I wouldn't be long covering it,' said I.

Judy Ryan let a laugh out of her as she put my dinner before me – stewed ribs, it was, with a plate of baked apples and cream to follow.

'Maybe it's a bike you want,' she teased. 'You'll be looking for a canal boat next.'

I attacked the stew. It was lovely. Plenty of sweet juicy pork on the ribs and with the potatoes just the way I liked them – some of them cooked to *briseach* to thicken the oniony gravy and more of them whole and firm.

'What's after putting the notion of a bike in your head, may I ask?' Gran brought her knitting over to the table and sat near me as I ate. She used to say that nothing gave her more pleasure than to watch me enjoying my food. I refused nothing, and I had an appetite like a bogman's.

I lowered the bone I was picking from my mouth.

'Oh, nothing,' I said casually. Then, a moment or two later: 'Mary Joe Heffernan and Bridie Murray have a new bike apiece.'

'H'mmm –' was Gran's comment. 'Isn't it well for them

153

that have money to burn?'

She said no more about the bike, and I never guessed a word of what she was up to, though it should have made me suspicious when she dressed herself and went into the town alone the following Saturday, for that was a thing she rarely did.

On the next Sunday week, Gran gave me a basket to take to an old crony of hers, Mrs. Doolin.

On Sunday evenings, I was often sent to call on bedridden Mrs. Doolin with small gifts of jelly and cake and snacks. If we had chicken for dinner, the cold breast was wrapped in butter-muslin and added to the contents of the brown basket with its lining of cool fresh cabbage leaves.

The invalid lived with her unmarried daughter in a small thatched cottage on the other side of Loughlin's Grove. I did not like going into the cottage which was dirty and ill-kept. If I went in, politeness forced me to accept the glass of buttermilk which Maria Doolin always offered. She was a sweaty untidy woman with dark greasy skin, heavy loose breasts and varicose legs. The thought that she had churned the buttermilk made it repugnant to me, and I hated to drink from the smeared glass which always smelled of dirty dishcloths.

I found it even more repugnant to enter the little room off the kitchen where Mrs. Doolin lay. The window had not been opened for twenty years and the fug of stale air, unwashed clothes and sickness was nauseating. To make matters worse, Mrs. Doolin always drew me down to her with a skinny claw and insisted on kissing me. My lips shrank from contact with her toothless mouth and bristling upper lip.

Whenever possible, I handed in the basket with a gabbled inquiry for Mrs. Doolin's health and, telling some lie about having to be home by a certain hour, I made a hasty escape.

There were compensations for these unpleasant visits.

In summer, there was joy in walking through the slowly gilding fields where corncrakes scolded in anger and tiny fieldmice clung precariously to swaying stalks of grain. In Loughlin's Grove, a narrow belt of wood which fringed the road opposite Doolin's, the mystery of the cool green shade was very pleasant. I sometimes lingered here when I had delivered my basket and spent an hour picking the sweet wild strawberries that grew so plentifully on the littly ferny hillocks in the Grove. To carry home the strawberries, I plucked long wiry stalks of wild wheat and threaded on to them the juicy red berries. Often, I brought home as many as ten hanks of strawberries.

I was forbidden to paddle in the stream that ran through the wood. Grandmother, who imposed so few restrictions on children's play, was unreasonable in her hatred of water. It dated from the time when my Aunt Alice, a child of six, had been found in the canal after having been missing for a day and a half. In Grandmother's trunk, carefully wrapped in tissue paper, were the little clothes Alice had been wearing that day. The clothes had never been washed – only dried and folded. I expect Gran felt that to wash them would be to lose the essence of contact with her child's body which the clothes retained. I had seen them once. Scraps of dried weeds from the canal's reedy bed still clung among the pleats of the stained little dress. In her prayer book Grandmother kept a strand of Alice's hair, a little golden circlet, unbelievably fine.

I am afraid I often ignored the ban which was placed on the stream. I could never resist the temptation to peel off shoes and stockings and dip my feet into the icy water, wriggling my toes luxuriously in the slimy black mud that lined the bed.

When bending over the stream I was always careful to keep my mouth tightly closed. Like all Ballyderrig children, I lived in mortal dread of the fat black tick-like creatures which we called darkie-lukers, and which were reputed to have a horrible tendency to leap from the water right into an open mouth. If you were so unlucky as to be invaded by a darkie-luker in this way, the only cure was to return to the stream on a moonlit night, and sit on the bank with your mouth open. It was believed that the sight of his fellows basking happily in the moonlit water might induce the fishy intruder to leave his human habitat through the door by which he had entered.

Personally, I never had much faith in this method of getting rid of a darkie-luker. I felt that, moon or no moon, to sit open-mouthed beside the stream was to ask for trouble.

It was barely possible that the black tick would jump out of your mouth, but it seemed to me just as likely that a whole shoal of darkie-lukers might be tempted to join their exiled brother. There was more sense in Judy Ryan's story of the Athy man who had got rid of one of these pests by standing, open-mouthed, over a pan of rasher gravy. The enticing smell of the gravy had lured the darkie-luker from his hiding-place.

But I started off to tell about that Sunday evening when Grandmother sent me to Mrs. Doolin with the flummery and cake. As I came home around the side of the house, swinging the empty basket, I heard a strange voice from the kitchen. Before opening the door, I looked in through the division in the curtains. Gran was there, sitting beside the fire in the big wooden chair with the red woollen cushions. Heck Murray was in the corner of the settle-bed drinking a big mug of tea. In the other corner of the settle, Judy Ryan and Mike Brophy sat side by side. Sitting before the fire was a visitor. His back was turned to me, but by his bald head I recognized him for Paddy Fitz, who kept the bicycle shop in the town.

I opened the door and went in, but once inside the door the power left my limbs and I could not have got out a word of greeting to save my life.

What was leaning against the dresser but a brand-new girl's bike!

Suddenly, I was struck with a wild fear that my joy might be premature or unfounded and that the bike might not really be for me. Dry-mouthed, I looked quickly at Gran.

She gave a little nod of her head and from her smile and the flush on her face it was plain that she was as pleased and excited as I was myself.

'Well?' she demanded. 'How do you like it?'

What could I say to her? Thank God for her understanding that let her see right into my heart and realize the love and joy and gratitude that were welling up there and were keeping me from thanking her in words.

'I wanted it to be a surprise for you,' she said. 'Paddy Fitz sent to Dublin specially for it. Sit up on it there till Paddy sees will he have to let down the saddle.'

'Did it cost a lot, Gran?' I asked later when the saddle had

been adjusted and every part of the bike down to the last tube of solution in the repair outfit had been examined and admired.

'Never you mind how much it cost,' Gran retorted. 'If it cost twice as much, I wasn't going to give Tommy Heffernan's daughter and Bridie Murray of the bog the laugh over you.'

James Plunkett (1920-   )
James Plunkett was born in 1920 in Dublin, the 'strumpet city' of most of
his stories and his two novels.
'Weep for Our Pride' comes from his collection of stories, *The Trusting
and the Maimed.* It is deliberately placed towards the end of *The Lucky Bag*
with those stories which could be called stepping-stones to the adult
world. Although there is harshness and cruelty in it, we recognise a
growing boy's courage and independence.

Weep for Our Pride
James Plunkett

THE DOOR OF THE CLASSROOM was opened by Mr. O'Rourke
just as Brother Quinlan was about to open it to leave. They
were both surprised and said 'Good morning' to one
another as they met in the doorway. Mr. O'Rourke,
although he met Brother Quinlan every morning of his life,
gave an expansive but oddly unreal smile and shouted his
good morning with blood-curdling cordiality. They then
withdrew to the passage outside to hold a conversation.

In the interval English Poetry books were opened and the
class began to repeat lines. They had been given the whole
of a poem called *Lament for the Death of Eoghan Roe* to learn. It
was very patriotic and dealt with the poisoning of Eoghan
Roe by the accursed English, and the lines were very long,
which made it difficult. The class hated the English for
poisoning Eoghan Roe because the lines about it were so
long. What made it worse was that it was the sort of poem
Mr. O'Rourke loved. If it was *Hail to thee blythe spirit* he
wouldn't be so fond of it. But he could declaim this one for
them in a rich, fruity, provincial baritone and would knock
hell out of anybody who had not learned it.

Peter had not learned it. Realising how few were the
minutes left to him he ran his eyes over stanza after stanza
and began to murmur fragments from each in hopeless
desperation. Swaine, who sat beside him, said, 'Do you
know this?'

159

'No,' Peter said, 'I haven't even looked at it.'

'My God!' Swaine breathed in horror. 'You'll be mangled!'

'You could give us a prompt.'

'And be torn limb from limb,' said Swaine with conviction; 'not likely.'

Peter closed his eyes. It was all his mother's fault. He had meant to come to school early to learn it but the row delayed him. It had been about his father's boots. After breakfast she had found that there were holes in both his shoes. She held them up to the light which was on because the November morning was wet and dark.

'Merciful God, child,' she exclaimed, 'there's not a sole in your shoes. You can't go out in those.'

He was anxious to put them on and get out quickly, but everybody was in bad humour. He didn't dare to say anything. His sister was clearing part of the table and his brother Joseph, who worked, was rooting in drawers and corners and growling to everybody.

'Where the hell is the bicycle pump? You can't leave a thing out of your hand in this house.'

'I can wear my sandals,' Peter suggested.

'And it spilling out of the heavens – don't be daft, child.' Then she said, 'What am I to do at all?'

For a moment he hoped he might be kept at home. But his mother told his sister to root among the old boots in the press. Millie went out into the passage. On her way she trod on the cat, which meowed in intense agony.

'Blazes,' said his sister, 'that bloody cat.'

She came in with an old pair of his father's boots, and he was made try them on. They were too big.

'I'm not going out in those,' he said, 'I couldn't walk in them.'

But his mother and sister said they looked lovely. They went into unconvincing ecstasies. They looked perfect they said, each backing up the other. No one would notice.

'They look foolish,' he insisted, 'I won't wear them.'

'You'll do what you're told,' his sister said. They were all older then he and each in turn bullied him. But the idea of being made look ridiculous nerved him.

'I won't wear them,' he persisted. At that moment his

160

brother Tom came in and Millie said quickly:

'Tom, speak to Peter – he's giving cheek to Mammy.'

Tom was very fond of animals. 'I heard the cat,' he began, looking threateningly at Peter who sometimes teased it. 'What were you doing to it?'

'Nothing,' Peter answered, 'Millie walked on it.' He tried to say something about the boots but the three of them told him to shut up and get to school. He could stand up to the others but he was afraid of Tom. So he had flopped along in the rain feeling miserable and hating it because people would be sure to know they were not his own boots.

The door opened and Mr. O'Rourke came in. He was a huge man in tweeds. He was a fluent speaker of Irish and wore the gold fáinne in the lapel of his jacket. Both his wrists were covered with matted black hair.

'*Filíocht*,' he roared and drew a leather from his hip pocket.

Then he shouted, '*Dún do leabhar*' and hit the front desk a ferocious crack with the leather. Mr. O'Rourke was an ardent Gael who gave his orders in Irish – even during English class. Someone had passed him up a poetry book and the rest closed theirs or turned them face downwards on their desks.

Mr. O'Rourke, his eyes glaring terribly at the ceiling, from which plaster would fall in fine dust when the third year students overhead tramped in or out, began to declaim:

> Did they dare, did they dare, to slay Eoghan Roe O'Neill?
> Yes they slew with poison him they feared to meet with steel.

He clenched his powerful fists and held them up rigidly before his chest.

> May God wither up their hearts, may their blood cease to flow!
> May they walk in living death who poisoned Eoghan Roe!

Then quite suddenly, in a business-like tone, he said, 'You – Daly.'

'Me, sir?' said Daly, playing for time.

161

'Yes, you fool,' thundered Mr. O'Rourke. 'You.'

Daly rose and repeated the first four lines. When he was half-way through the second stanza Mr. O'Rourke bawled, 'Clancy.' Clancy rose and began to recite. They stood up and sat down as Mr. O'Rourke commanded while he paced up and down the aisles between the seats. Twice he passed close to Peter. He stood for some time by Peter's desk bawling out names. The end of his tweed jacket lay hypnotically along the edge of Peter's desk. Cummins stumbled over the fourth verse and dried up completely.

'Line,' Mr. O'Rourke bawled. Cummins, calmly pale, left his desk and stepped out to the side of the class. Two more were sent out. Mr. O'Rourke walked up and down once more and stood with his back to Peter. Looking at the desk at the very back he suddenly bawled, 'Farrell.'

Peter's heart jerked. He rose to his feet. The back was still towards him. He looked at it, a great mountain of tweed, with a frayed collar over which the thick neck bulged in folds. He could see the antennae of hair which sprouted from Mr. O'Rourke's ears and could smell the chalk-and-ink schoolmaster's smell from him. It was a trick of Mr. O'Rourke's to stand with his back to you and then call your name. It made the shock more unnerving. Peter gulped and was silent.

'Wail....' prompted Mr. O'Rourke.

Peter said, 'Wail....'

Mr. O'Rourke paced up to the head of the class once more.

'Wail – wail him through the island,' he said as he walked. Then he turned around suddenly and said, 'Well, go on.'

'Wail, wail him through the island,' Peter said once more and stopped.

'Weep,' hinted Mr. O'Rourke.

He regarded Peter closely, his eyes narrowing.

'Weep,' said Peter, ransacking the darkness of his mind but finding only emptiness.

'Weep, weep, weep,' Mr. O'Rourke said, his voice rising.

Peter chanced his arm. He said, 'Wail, wail him through the island, weep, weep, weep.'

Mr. O'Rourke stood up straight. His face conveyed at once shock, surprise, pain.

'Get out to the line,' he roared, 'you thick lazy good-for-nothing bloody imbecile. Tell him what it is, Clancy.' Clancy dithered for a moment, closed his eyes and said:

Sir – Wail, wail him through the island, weep, weep for
  our pride
Would that on the battle field our gallant chief had
  died.

Mr. O'Rourke nodded with dangerous benevolence. As Peter shuffled to the line the boots caught the iron upright of the desk and made a great clamour. Mr. O'Rourke gave him a cut with the leather across the behind. 'Did you look at this, Farrell?' he asked.

Peter hesitated and said uncertainly, 'No, sir.'

'It wasn't worth your while, I suppose?'

'No, sir. I hadn't time, sir.'

Just then the clock struck the hour. The class rose. Mr. O'Rourke put the leather under his left armpit and crossed himself. '*In ainm an athar*,' he began. While they recited the *Hail Mary* Peter, unable to pray, stared at the leafless rain-soaked trees in the square and the serried rows of pale, prayerful faces. They sat down.

Mr. O'Rourke turned to the class.

'Farrell hadn't time,' he announced pleasantly. Then he looked thunderously again at Peter. 'If it was an English penny dreadful about Public Schools or London crime you'd find time to read it quick enough, but when it's about the poor hunted martyrs and felons of your own unfortunate country by a patriot like Davis you've no time for it. You've the makings of a fine little Britisher.' With genuine pathos Mr. O'Rourke then recited:

The weapon of the Sassenach met him on his way
And he died at Cloch Uachter upon St. Leonard's day.

'That was the dear dying in any case, but if he died for the likes of you, Farrell, it was the dear bitter dying, no mistake about it.'

Peter said, 'I meant to learn it.'

'Hold out your hand. If I can't preach respect for the patriot dead into you, then honest to my stockings I'll beat respect into you. Hand.'

Peter held it out. He pulled his coat sleeve down over his wrist. The leather came down six times with a resounding impact. He tried to keep his thumb out of the way because if it hit you on the thumb it stung unbearably. But after four heavy slaps the hand began to curl of its own accord, curl and cripple like a piece of tin-foil in a fire, until the thumb lay powerless across the palm, and the pain burned in his chest and constricted every muscle. But worse than the pain was the fear that he would cry. He was turning away when Mr. O'Rourke said:

'Just a moment, Farrell. I haven't finished.'

Mr. O'Rourke gently took the fingers of Peter's hand, smoothing them out as he drew them once more into position. 'To teach you I'll take no defiance,' he said, in a friendly tone and raised the leather. Peter tried to hold his crippled hand steady.

He could not see properly going back to his desk and again the boots deceived him and he tripped and fell. As he picked himself up Mr. O'Rourke, about to help him with another, though gentler, tap of the leather, stopped and exclaimed:

'Merciful God, child, where did you pick up the boots?'

The rest looked with curiosity. Clancy, who had twice excelled himself, tittered. Mr. O'Rourke said, 'And what's the funny joke, Clancy?'

'Nothing, sir.'

'Soft as a woman's was your voice, O'Neill, bright was your eye,' recited Mr. O'Rourke, in a voice as soft as a woman's, brightness in his eyes. 'Continue, Clancy.' But Clancy, the wind taken out of his sails, missed and went out to join the other three. Peter put his head on the desk, his raw hands tightly under his armpits, and nursed his wounds while the leather thudded patriotism and literature into the other, unmurmuring, four.

Swaine said nothing for a time. Now and then he glanced at Peter's face. He was staring straight at the book. His hands were tender, but the pain had ebbed away. Each still hid its rawness under a comfortably warm armpit.

'You got a heck of a hiding,' Swaine whispered at last. Peter said nothing.

'Ten is too much. He's not allowed to give you ten. If he

164

gave me ten I'd bring my father up to him.'

Swaine was small, but his face was large and bony and when he took off his glasses sometimes to wipe them there was a small red weal on the bridge of his nose. Peter grunted and Swaine changed the subject.

'Tell us who owns the boots. They're not your own.'

'Yes they are,' Peter lied.

'Go on,' Swaine said, 'who owns them? Are they your brother's?'

'Shut up,' Peter menaced.

'Tell us,' Swaine persisted. 'I won't tell a soul. Honest.' He regarded Peter with sly curiosity. He whispered: 'I know they're not your own, but I wouldn't tell it. We sit beside one another. We're pals. You can tell me.'

'Curiosity killed the cat ...' Peter said.

Swaine had the answer to that. With a sly grin he rejoined, 'Information made him fat.'

'If you must know,' Peter said, growing tired, 'they're my father's. And if you tell anyone I'll break you up in little pieces. You just try breathing a word.'

Swaine sat back, satisfied.

Mr. O'Rourke was saying that the English used treachery when they poisoned Eoghan Roe. But what could be expected of the English except treachery?

'Hoof of the horse,' he quoted, 'Horn of a bull, smile of a Saxon.' Three perils. Oliver Cromwell read his Bible while he quartered infants at their mothers' breasts. People said let's forget all that. But we couldn't begin to forget it until we had our full freedom. Our own tongue, the sweet Gaelic *teanga*, must be restored once more as the spoken language of our race. It was the duty of all to study and work towards that end.

'And those of us who haven't time must be shown how to find the time. Isn't that a fact, Farrell?' he said. The class laughed. But the clock struck and Mr. O'Rourke put the lament regretfully aside.

'Mathematics,' he announced, '*Céimseachta.*'

He had hoped it would continue to rain during lunch-time so that they could stay in the classroom. But when the automatic bell clanged loudly and Mr. O'Rourke opened the frosted window to look out, it had stopped. They trooped down the stairs. They pushed and jostled one another. Peter kept his hand for safety on the banisters. Going down the stairs made the boots seem larger. He made straight for the urinal and stayed there until the old brother whose duty it was for obscure moral reasons to patrol the place had passed through twice. The second time he said to him: 'My goodness, boy, go out into the fresh air with your playmates. Shoo – boy – shoo,' and stared at Peter's retreating back with perplexity and suspicion.

Dillon came over as he was unwrapping his lunch and said, 'Did they dare, did they dare to slay Eoghan Roe O'Neill.'

'Oh, shut up,' Peter said.

Dillon linked his arm and said, 'You got an awful packet.' Then with genuine admiration he added: 'You took it super. He aimed for your wrist, too. Not a peek. You were wizard. Cripes. When I saw him getting ready for the last four I was praying you wouldn't cry.'

'I never cried yet,' Peter asserted.

'I know, but he lammed his hardest. You shouldn't have said you hadn't time.'

'He wouldn't make me cry,' Peter said grimly, 'not if he got up at four o'clock in the morning to try it.'

O'Rourke had lammed him all right, but there was no use trying to do anything about it. If he told his father and mother they would say he richly deserved it. It was his mother should have been lammed and not he.

'You were super, anyway,' Dillon said warmly. They walked arm in arm. 'The Irish,' he added sagaciously, 'are an unfortunate bloody race. The father often says so.'

'Don't tell me,' Peter said with feeling.

'I mean, look at us. First Cromwell knocks hell out of us for being too Irish and then Rorky slaughters us for not being Irish enough.'

It was true. It was a pity they couldn't make up their minds.

Peter felt the comfort of Dillon's friendly arm. 'The boots are my father's,' he confided suddenly, 'my own had holes.' That made him feel better.

'What are you worrying about?' Dillon said, reassuringly. 'They look all right to me.'

166

When they were passing the row of water taps with the chained drinking vessels a voice cried, 'There's Farrell now.' A piece of crust hit Peter on the nose.

'Caesar sends his legate,' Dillon murmured. They gathered round. Clancy said, 'Hey, boys, Farrell is wearing someone else's boots.'

'Who lifted you into them?'

'Wait now,' said Clancy, 'let's see him walk. Go on – walk, Farrell.'

Peter backed slowly towards the wall. He backed slowly until he felt the ridge of a downpipe hard against his back. Dillon came with him. 'Lay off, Clancy,' Dillon said. Swaine was there too. He was smiling, a small cat fat with information.

'Where did you get them, Farrell?'

'Pinched them.'

'Found them in an ashbin.'

'Make him walk,' Clancy insisted; 'let's see you walk, Farrell.'

'They're my own,' Peter said; 'they're a bit big – that's all.'

'Come on, Farrell – tell us whose they are.'

The grins grew wider.

Clancy said, 'They're his father's.'

'No, they're not,' Peter denied quickly.

'Yes, they are. He told Swaine. Didn't he, Swaine? He told you they were his father's.'

Swaine's grin froze. Peter fixed on him with terrible eyes.

'Well, didn't he, Swaine? Go on, tell the chaps what he told you. Didn't he say they were his father's?'

Swaine edged backwards. 'That's right,' he said, 'he did.'

'Hey, you chaps,' Clancy said, impatiently, 'let's make him walk. I vote...'

At that moment Peter, with a cry, sprang on Swaine. His fist smashed the glasses on Swaine's face. As they rolled over on the muddy ground, Swaine's nails tore his cheek. Peter saw the white terrified face under him. He beat at it in frenzy until it became covered with mud and blood.

'Cripes,' Clancy said in terror, 'look at Swaine's glasses. Haul him off, lads.' They pulled him away and he lashed out at them with feet and hands. He lashed out awkwardly with the big boots which had caused the trouble. Swaine's nose and lips were bleeding so they took him over to the water tap and washed him. Dillon, who stood alone with Peter, brushed his clothes as best he could and fixed his collar and tie.

'You broke his glasses,' he said. 'There'll be a proper rucky if old Quinny sees him after lunch.'

'I don't care about Quinny.'

'I do then,' Dillon said fervently. 'He'll quarter us all in our mother's arms.'

They sat with their arms folded while Brother Quinlan, in the high chair at the head of the class, gave religious instruction. Swaine kept his bruised face lowered. Without the glasses it had a bald, maimed look, as though his eyebrows, or a nose, or an eye, were missing. They had exchanged no words since the fight. Peter was aware of the boots. They were a defeat, something to be ashamed of. His mother only thought they would keep out the rain. She didn't understand that it would be better to have wet feet. People did not laugh at you because your feet were wet.

Brother Quinlan was speaking of our relationship to one another, of the boy to his neighbour and of the boy to his God. We communicated with one another, he said, by looks, gestures, speech. But these were surface contacts. They conveyed little of what went on in the mind, and nothing at all of the individual soul. Inside us, the greatest and the humblest of us, a whole world was locked. Even if we tried we could convey nothing of that interior world, that life which was nourished, as the poet had said, within the brain. In our interior life we stood without a friend or ally – alone. In the darkness and silence of that interior and eternal world the immortal soul and its God were at all times face to face. No one else could peer into another's soul, neither our teacher, nor our father or mother, nor even our best friend. But God saw all. Every stray little thought which moved in that inaccessible world was as plain to Him as if it were thrown across the bright screen of a cinema. That was why we must be as careful to discipline our thoughts as our actions. Custody of the eyes, custody of the ears, but above all else custody....

Brother Quinlan let the sentence trail away and fixed his eyes on Swaine.

'You – boy,' he said in a voice which struggled to be patient, 'what are you doing with that handkerchief?'

Swaine's nose had started to bleed again. He said nothing. 'Stand up, boy,' Brother Quinlan commanded. He had glasses himself, which he wore during class on the tip of his nose. He was a big man too, and his head was bald in front, which made his large forehead appear even more massive. He stared over the glasses at Swaine.

'Come up here,' he said, screwing up his eyes, the fact that something was amiss with Swaine's face dawning gradually on him. Swaine came up to him, looking woe-begone, still dabbing his nose with the handkerchief.

Brother Quinlan contemplated the battered face for some time. He turned to the class.

'Whose handiwork is this?' he asked quietly. 'Stand up, the boy responsible for this.'

For a while nobody stirred. There was an uneasy stillness. Poker faces looked at the desks in front of them and waited. Peter looked around and saw Dillon gazing at him hopefully. After an unbearable moment feet shuffled and Peter stood up.

'I am, sir,' he said.

Brother Quinlan told Clancy to take Swaine out to the yard to bathe his nose. Then he spoke to the class about violence and what was worse, violence to a boy weaker than oneself. That was the resort of the bully and the scoundrel – physical violence – The Fist. At this Brother Quinlan held up his large bunched fist so that all might see it. Then with the other hand he indicated to the picture of the Sacred Heart. Charity and Forebearance, he said, not vengeance and intolerance, those were qualities most dear to Our Blessed Lord.

'Are you not ashamed of yourself, Farrell? Do you think what you have done is a heroic or a creditable thing?'

'No, sir,'

'Then why did you do it, boy?'

Peter made no answer. It was no use making an answer. It was no use saying Swaine had squealed about the boots being his father's. Swaine's face was badly battered. But deep inside him Peter felt battered too. Brother Quinlan couldn't see your soul. He could see Swaine's face, though, when he fixed his glasses on him properly. Brother Quinlan took his silence for defiance.

'A blackguardly affair,' he pronounced. 'A low, cowardly assault. Hold out your hand.'

Peter hesitated. There was a limit. He hadn't meant not to learn the poetry and it wasn't his fault about the boots.

'He's been licked already, sir,' Dillon said. 'Mr. O'Rourke gave him ten.'

'Mr. O'Rourke is a discerning man,' said Brother Quinlan, 'but he doesn't seem to have given him half enough. Think of the state of that poor boy who has just gone out.'

Peter could think of nothing to say. He tried hard but there were no words there. Reluctantly he presented his hand. It was mudstained. Brother Quinlan looked at it with distaste. Then he proceeded to beat hell out of him, and charity and forebearance into him, in the same way as Mr. O'Rourke earlier had hammered in patriotism and respect for Irish History.

It was raining again when he was going home. Usually there were three or four to go home with him, but this afternoon he went alone. He did not want them with him. He passed some shops and walked by the first small suburban gardens, with their sodden gravel paths and dripping gates. On the canal bridge a boy passed him pushing fuel in a pram. His feet were bare. The mud had splashed upwards in thick streaks to his knees. Peter kept his hand under his coat. There was a blister on the ball of the thumb which ached now like a burn. Brother Quinlan did that. He probably didn't aim to hit the thumb as Mr. O'Rourke always did, but his sight was so bad he had a rotten shot. The boots had got looser than they were earlier. He realised this when he saw Clancy with three or four others passing on the other side of the road. When Clancy waved and called to him, he backed automatically until he felt the parapet against his back.

'Hey, Farrell,' they called. Then one of them, his head forward, his behind stuck out, began to waddle with grotesque movements up the road. The rest yelled to call Peter's attention. They indicated the mime. Come back if you like, they shouted. Peter waited until they had gone. Then he turned moodily down the bank of the canal. He walked with a stiff ungainly dignity, his mind not yet quite made up. Under the bridge the water was deep and narrow, and a raw wind which moaned in the high arch whipped coldly at his face. It might rain tomorrow and his shoes wouldn't be mended. If his mother thought the boots were all right God knows when his shoes would be mended. After a moment of indecision he took off the boots and dropped them, first one – and then the other – into the water.

There would be hell to pay when he came home without them. But there would be hell to pay anyway when Swaine's father sent around the note to say he had broken young Swaine's glasses. Like the time he broke the Cassidy's window. Half regretfully he stared at the silty water. He could see his father rising from the table to reach for the belt which hung behind the door. The outlook was frightening; but it was better to walk in your bare feet. It was better to walk without shoes and barefooted than to walk without dignity. He took off his stockings and stuffed them into his pocket. His heart sank as he felt the cold wet mud of the path on his bare feet.

Polly Devlin (1944-   )
Polly Devlin is one of a family of six sisters and one brother who grew up
in County Tyrone. She has recently published an autobiographical
account of those years under the title *All of us there*, and her first
children's book is *The Far Side of the Lough*, whose stories are based on a
real place called Ardboe and the real people who surrounded her when
she was growing up.
Good children's writers have never shied away from difficult themes,
and in this story, 'The China Doll', Polly Devlin's theme is the grown-up
betrayal of the child and the subsequent loss of trust. The story is
compellingly yet cleverly told so that the shock at the end of the story is
bearable because it is related at second hand.

The China Doll
Polly Devlin

MY MOTHER DIED when I was a little girl and Mary-Ellen
Martin came to look after me. She had red hair, and
speckled eyes and a face that was brown with freckles, and
she always wore a flowery cross-over overall tied at the
back, except on Sundays when she wore what she called her
Costume which was a grey suit with a pleated skirt and a
blouse. She wore wellingtons when she went outside the
back door to feed the hens, or to get water from the pump
or, when the pump broke, as it often did, to draw water up
from the well.

Inside the house, in the kitchen and scullery, with their
flagstone floors that she scrubbed every day, she wore
plimsolls, only she called them gutties. She always went
bare-legged in summer except when she was going to
worship, for there were no such things as tights then and
stockings were expensive.

In the winter Mary-Ellen wore men's socks and when she
ran outside to feed the hens or collect eggs or to get coal or
water, her legs became covered in goose-pimples which she
called warbles. Whenever I was naughty she always said
she'd beat me so hard she would leave my legs in warbles.

But she never hit me in her life.

The thing I loved more than almost anything was for Mary-Ellen to tell me stories about when she was a little girl, the youngest of seven children and living in a two-roomed house on the shores of Lough Neagh, the biggest lake in Ireland.

The place where she lived was called Ardboe, which meant High Cow in Irish. There was an old ruined abbey there, near where she lived, and beside it a High Cross, built a thousand years before, and still standing because its mortar had been mixed with the milk of a magic cow that lived on the hill where the Cross stood. 'So it was the High Cow,' Mary-Ellen said, 'and one bad night some bad men who coveted the cow and its magic powers came and made off with the beast and stole it away. When the monks came the next morning, there was no cow and nowhere to find it. As they were mourning the loss, they saw that on the stones, by the side of the lough, there was the imprint of the cow's hoof. They followed the markings and it led them far away to where the cow was hid, and they took her back, and finished the Cross and there it still is and if you walk up to Golloman's Point,' Mary-Ellen said, 'and you know where to look, you can see still the stone with a hoof mark in it, from when she left her trail.'

I knew that Mary-Ellen's house was near Golloman's Point, where the charming man lived, and that it was set back from a road called the Car Road and that the lane that led to her house was called a loanin. When Mary-Ellen first told me the name of the road and I said, surprised, 'But Mary-Ellen there were no cars in your day,' she laughed at me saying 'your day' like that and explained that car meant any four-wheeled vehicle.

Mary-Ellen's house was small and low with thick mud walls, whitewashed every year, and a black rim painted along the bottom to hide splashes and mud marks. The roof was corrugated iron, painted bright green, and the rain, Mary-Ellen said, rattled on it as though someone was clodding stones at it. There were two rooms in the house, the kitchen and the bedroom, which Mary-Ellen always called the Room when she was telling me about it. There was no lavatory, no bathroom, and nowhere to go if you

173

wanted to be alone. There were five beds in the bedroom and Mary-Ellen, as the smallest child, slept in the truckle bed that was kept under her parents' bed.

There was no electricity then and though they got paraffin oil lamps when Mary-Ellen was older, when she was a little girl, the same age as me, the only light for the evenings and nights were tallow candles which her mother made by dipping rushes into animal fat. They gave a flickering, dim light, but since there were no books to read, and as Mary-Ellen's sisters and mother could knit without looking at what they were doing, that frail light was not a problem.

Two or three evenings neighbours would call in for what they called a crack – an evening's talk, sitting around the flickering fire in the half-light, telling ghost stories. Mary-Ellen was afraid to go out of the house in the evening after hearing about the banshees and the ghosts and the black dogs that everyone had met, and when she had to run down to the closet at the end of the little garden at the back of the house, called the rampar, she ran quickly with her eyes closed.

There was no wireless either in Mary-Ellen's house. The only music she ever heard as a child was when, instead of a crack, there was a ceili; then, the neighbours brought along a melodeon or a mouth-organ or a fiddle, and John-Joe, Mary-Ellen's oldest brother, played his accordion and the men sang the old songs, which were laments and comeallyes.

'They were called that because they always started with the words: Come-all-ye-lads and lassies...' Mary-Ellen said, and she would start to sing one for me.

When Mary-Ellen was growing up she rarely saw a real car, what we would call a car. There were very few horses since the farms were small and the fields were dug by hand, and the men rowed their boats out on to the lough, for there were no engines.

Whenever my father brought back any food that was different from our usual food, from his visits to other countries or to the city, Mary-Ellen would exclaim about it and examine it suspiciously. When she was a little girl the food had been very simple and she seldom ate meat, but there was usually plenty of fish, particularly eels, because

174

their father earned his living as a fisherman.

Schools were closed for two weeks in October so that the children could help their families with the potato harvest, and potatoes were by far the most important part of their food. Every evening Packy, Mary-Ellen's second oldest brother, would fetch milk in two tin cans from where the Martins' cow was milked at the house a bit farther up the road, where the water-well was too. There was always froth on the milk in one of the cans, milked straight from the cow, and Mary-Ellen's mother skimmed it off for the hens; the buttermilk in the other she used for the flat scones of soda bread, called farls, that she made every day.

With seven children Mary-Ellen's mother needed to bake a lot of bread and to do a huge washing every day. Every drop of water had to be carried from the farm well (called Maggie's Well) and every griddleful of soda bread was baked on the stove that had to be kept full of wood or coal from morning to night and needed to be riddled free of ashes hourly.

All the children worked hard in the house, in the tiny garden, on the lough, and especially at the harvest and potato-picking times on the neighbouring farms. The hens lived in a pen in the rampar behind the house but none of Mary-Ellen's family ate their eggs. They were sold so that Mary-Ellen's mother could get money for the children's shoes for wearing on Sundays.

The kitchen where everyone ate and spent their working hours when they weren't out of doors, or at school, was small and dark and warm, with red tiles on the floor. There was an iron stove, with a pipe for the smoke, curving into the wall, with a rack above for clothes, and above that again a shelf with a deckled brass edging, and the ornaments on that only came down to be washed or dusted once a year.

Though I had never seen Mary-Ellen's house I felt I knew it better than my own; and everything on that shelf I knew by heart, for I had made Mary-Ellen recite so often how she helped her mother to take the ornaments down, holding them carefully and holding her breath: two brown china alsatian dogs that her father had won at a fair; two vases with fluted white frilly edges and flowers painted on; a clock with a humpy back; and two willow-pattern plates that an old

175

man called Forbie had given them. We had willow-pattern plates too and I was very pleased about that.

The stove was used for heating the house as well as for cooking and early every morning Mary-Ellen's mother got up first, riddled out the old dead ashes, and lit a new fire. One of Mary-Ellen's jobs was to carry in coal and to collect sticks for kindling. She put these under the stove to dry where their dog often lay.

There was a big wooden settle near to the stove where the children sat, and a big chair on the other side which was kept for their father. There was a dresser with drawers and shelves and on its lowest shelf were the soda farls baked that day and next to it the two buckets covered with wooden lids with all the water for the house, brought up by John-Joe or Packy who carried them on a yoke slung over the shoulders.

By the window was a scrubbed table where the family ate but it was too small for them all to sit at all at once and so the younger children took their food over to the settle by the fire and ate it there.

Mary-Ellen remembered being very hungry in the winter when the lough was too rough to go fishing. 'We lived as best we could on the potatoes we stored in pits in the autumn, and any cabbage and leeks we had in our own wee garden.' Winter or summer, though, the older children had to help to gather bait for fishing lines, and Mary-Ellen used to feel sorry for her sisters some mornings when their mother roused them for school and they were still tired from the night before when they had stumbled through the damp darkness with only a hand-made lantern (a candle in a jam-jar tied up with string) to guide them as they gathered worms for bait.

Their clothes were hand-me-downs from each other and other people, and although their mother knitted as much as she could, she had little time for sewing or knitting. Mary-Ellen and her sisters knitted all the socks for themselves and their father and brothers, and did the darning. There was no money for games or toys, and the children made their own pastimes and the only bought toys that Mary-Ellen remembered, until the day the parcel came, was a football that the boys had saved for, and the bouncing balls the girls played with at school. All else was carved or whittled. Mary-

Ellen had a wooden cat made by John-Joe. He'd carved a round head and a body and arms, all from one piece of wood, and her biggest sister Kathleen had knitted a cover for the cat's dark, hard body.

Behind her back the family called her cat the Tackle, which was what her father called anything or anybody that got in his way, or that he wanted to scold or to make fun of. He didn't like the dog being in the house and if he spied it under the stove he'd shout, 'Come out of there, you tackle, and bad cess to you,' or if Mary-Ellen had left her cat on the table or on his chair he would say, 'Get that tackle out of my sight.'

Mary-Ellen wanted to call her cat Bernadette after the saint but her mother said it wouldn't be right. The wooden cat was the only toy she had so she carried it with her where and when she could.

One day the postman came to the door of the house with a parcel addressed to The Martin Family. Mary-Ellen said she'd never forget it to her dying day, how the postman came in and put the parcel on the table over by the window. The postman rarely called at their house. Sometimes he came in, with what he called a letter-with-a-window, which was an official letter, about her father's fishing licence, or at Christmas he delivered a few treasured cards from relatives in America or England. But this time he brought in a big parcel, covered with stamps.

Mary-Ellen and her mother stood and stared at it for a long time after the postman had gone. They turned it round and on one side was the name and address of the sender – Mrs. Chandler, Fort Ticonderoga, N.Y., U.S.A.

'Mrs. Chandler,' said Mary-Ellen's mother, 'is our May-Ellie, my eldest sister.' She had emigrated to the United States years before, long before Mary-Ellen was born, while her mother was still a little girl herself. They hadn't heard from her in years, not even a card at Christmas.

'Are you for opening it?' Mary-Ellen asked her mother. Her father was on the lough and her brothers were out at school and so were her sisters. Mary-Ellen told me that she was as afraid that her mother would say yes as she was that she would say no. Whichever she did was going to make Mary-Ellen feel nervous and desperate, either with excitement or with waiting. Her mother said wait, wait till the father got home. Mary-Ellen waited in the garden, near the gate, watching for him, hoping that he'd get home before school home-coming time, so that she could see into the parcel before her sisters and brothers were there to take what she wanted, as they always did, because they were bigger and older.

But they came down the road first and she ran towards them, shouting, so that they began to run towards her, frightened by her voice, alarmed at what might have happened, and when they could make it out, they rushed into the house and crowded around the table, looking at the parcel. But until their father came in they couldn't open it. Their mother tried to get them to lay the table, or to help her redd up the kitchen, but though they did try to help, their hearts weren't in it. They kept looking out of the door for their father.

When at last they saw him coming up from the lough, they didn't run towards him shouting, for fear it would anger or frighten him. Instead John-Joe went to meet him, to tell him the news and he ran in too and went straight over to the parcel and got out the knife he used to cut and trim the worms and hooks and lines, and parted the string. Their mother saved the stamps, and the string, and the first wrapping of paper inside the box which was an American newspaper. Inside of that was another big box and when that was opened there was white tissue-paper around a man's suit of clothes.

Underneath that, in bundles and packages, was a set of clothes for every child, with labels and names. Mary-Ellen's mother kept saying, as they were lifted out one by one – a red pleated skirt like a kilt for Kathleen, a blue dress with a white collar for Bridget, a blue skirt with pleats and braces for Teresa, and white rabbits embroidered on the waistband, check waistcoats and trousers for the boys – half laughing and half crying, 'How is it that our Ellie knows all our ones' names and ages so well? What's come over her sending us all this, and never a word from her these years?'

There was a white wooly coat for Mary-Ellen, that felt somewhat like fur, and each girl had a pair of white ankle-socks with a pattern round the tops. That was the first time

Mary-Ellen had ever seen ankle-socks, for all the girls wore black knitted stockings at that time. There was a knitted jacket and blouse and skirt for their mother. Then, when everyone had got their parcels, there at the very bottom of the box was another box with Mary-Ellen's name on it. Her mother lifted it out and gave it to Mary-Ellen without opening it. Mary-Ellen was afraid to open it. Her brothers and sisters were all watching her in a ring, and her mother and father standing behind them, but they said go on, and she went down on her hunkers and opened the box. There was tissue-paper and a card on the top and on it was written: 'To one Mary-Ellen from another' and her mother read it out and said, 'Our May-Ellie's name was by rights Mary-Ellen, the same as you. I called you after her.'

Then Mary-Ellen opened the tissue-paper which had light gold stars printed on it. And inside the paper a doll was lying, with golden curly hair and closed eyes with black lashes and a white dress, white socks, black shoes and a necklace round her neck. Mary-Ellen looked at the doll, and sighed.

Her mother said, 'Lift it out,' and Mary-Ellen put her hands into the paper and lifted the doll out, and as she did so, the doll's eyes opened wide, as blue as blue, said Mary-Ellen. She would never forget it looking back at her. She nearly dropped the doll but still no one spoke. Then Mary-Ellen said , 'Is it mine?'

'It is yours,' her mother said.

'And can I keep it?' Mary-Ellen said.

Whenever she got to this part of her story, her voice always got higher and smaller, and she would look away blinking, and so would I, trying not to cry for her and me and the doll and the moment and for what I knew she had been feeling. And when her mother said, 'You can so, it's yours,' and Philomena the sister just older than Mary-Ellen began to cry for wanting it, Mary-Ellen knew it was hers, and everyone began talking.

The girls all wanted to look at the doll, but at the same time they wanted to try on their new clothes. Their mother went into the room to put on the new jacket and skirt and the white blouse with its high neck, and when she came out everyone stared at her and their father put his hand on her shoulder in a way Mary-Ellen had never seen before. And then all the sisters and brothers except Mary-Ellen ran in to put on *their* new clothes, and at the very end, their father went into the room, and put on the new suit, and when he came out, they all clapped him and themselves and their mother.

Mary-Ellen was still kneeling, holding her doll and watching, and laughing, and her mother bent down and told her to let Philomena hold the doll till she changed into her new coat. She didn't want to, in case she never got the doll back.

'Any other time,' Mary-Ellen said, 'I would have been over the moon about the white coat – but I could only think of the doll and I was out of that room and changed like the Creggan White Hare, to get the doll back from Philomena.'

Then their mother said, 'There's going to be no tea the night with all this consate and admiring, away into the room and out of your new clothes, the fire will be dead on us.'

And so slowly they all changed back into their old clothes and sat down to eat, although Mary-Ellen could hardly eat.

The next morning, when she woke early, the doll was still there. When all the rest of the family had gone to school or work she played with it, and talked to it while her mother cooked and baked. And then her mother got out a bottle of ink and paper, to write to her aunt about the parcel, and she told Mary-Ellen to play outside for a while. Mary-Ellen stayed by the gate hoping somebody would pass so she could show them her new doll, but no one passed by. The Car Road was empty and still, except for one man, some distance down the road, standing on steps, clipping a hedge with shears. Mary-Ellen knew who he was, though she had never spoken to him, being a shy child, but she opened her gate, and went down to him, holding her doll carefully and stood at the front of his steps. He did not stop in his work, nor look at her, so she called up that she had a new doll, it had come from America with her name on it.

The man stopped clipping the hedge and listened, and then leaned down and said, 'Show us the doll,' and Mary-Ellen handed it up, smiling. He took it and looked at it for a time, and then came down the steps and put the doll on the top step and took his shears in both hands and cut its head off.

The head fell at Mary-Ellen's feet, its hair still curly, its blue eyes wide open; the body fell on the other side of the steps. Mary-Ellen saw the head and the separate body but her voice had gone, as though it too had been severed. She could not speak. The man climbed up the steps again and began to clip the hedge. After a while Mary-Ellen's mother came to see where she was, and found her, mute, in the ditch, with the two pieces of her doll. Something more than a doll had been broken, Mary-Ellen said with a sigh. She never had another doll in her life.

James Stephens (1880 or 1882-1950)
James Stephens was born – or so he thought – on 2 February 1882, in
Dublin, the same day as his friend in later years, James Joyce. In
everyday life he worked as a solicitor's clerk in the Dublin of Yeats and
AE (George Russell). In 1912 he published *The Crock of Gold* of which
Walter de la Mare was to say: 'Like half the best books it is more than a
little mad, and is crammed full of life and beauty.'
More than a little mad and full of irony too is the 'fairy' tale included
here, 'The Unworthy Princess'. It is from his collection of stories
published in 1913 under the title *Here Are Ladies* and is a true fable, in
that it can be enjoyed on many levels. Stephens clearly understood the
fantastic logic of childhood.

The Unworthy Princess

James Stephens

HIS MOTHER FINISHED READING the story of the Beautiful
Princess, and it was surely the saddest story he had ever
heard. He could not bear to think of that lovely and delicate
lady all alone in the huge, black castle, waiting, waiting until
the giant came back from killing her seven brothers. He
would come back with their seven heads swinging pitifully
from his girdle, and when he reached the castle he would
gnash his teeth through the keyhole with a noise like the
grinding together of great rocks, and would poke his head
through the fanlight of the door and say fee-faw-fum in a
voice of such exceeding loudness that the castle would be
shaken to its foundations.

Thinking of this his throat grew painful with emotion, and
his heart swelled to the most uncomfortable dimensions,
and he resolved to devote his whole life to the rescue of the
Princess and, if necessary, die in her defence.

Such was his impatience that he could wait for nothing
more than his dinner, and this he ate so speedily as to cause
his father to call him a Perfect-Young-Glutton and a
Disgrace-To-Any-Table. He bore these insults in a meek and
heroic spirit, whereupon his mother said he was ill, and it

183

was only by a sustained and violent outcry that he escaped being sent to bed.

Immediately after dinner, he set out in search of the Giant's-Castle. Now, a Giant's-Castle is one of the most difficult things in the world to find; that is because it is so large that one can only see it through the wrong end of a telescope, and further, he did not even know this giant's name; and so he might never have found the way if he had not met a certain Old-Woman on the common. She was a very nice Old-Woman: she had three teeth and a red shawl, and an umbrella with groceries inside it; so he told her of the difficulty he was in. She replied that he was in luck's way, and that she was the only person in the world who could assist him. She said her name was Really-and-Truly, and that she had a magic head, and that if he cut off her head it would answer any questions he asked it. So he stropped his penknife on his boot and said he was ready. The Old-Woman then told him that in all affairs of this delicate nature it was customary to take the will for the deed, and that he might now ask her head anything he wanted to know, so he asked the head what was the way to the nearest giant, and the head replied that if he took the first turning to the left, the second to the right and then the first to the left again, and knocked at the fifth door on the right-hand side, he would see the giant.

He thanked the Old-Woman very much for the use of her head, and she permitted him to lend her one threepenny piece, one pocket handkerchief, one gun-metal watch, and one bootlace. She said that she never took two of anything because that was not fair, and that she wanted these for a very particular secret purpose about which she dare not speak and as to which she trusted he would not press her, and then she took a most affectionate leave of him and went away.

He followed her directions with the utmost fidelity and soon found himself opposite a house which, to the eye of anyone over seven years of age, looked very like any other house, but to the searching eye of six and three-quarters it was palpably and patently a Giant's-Castle. He tried the door, but it was locked, as, indeed, he expected it would be, and then he crept very cautiously and peeped through the

first-floor window. He could see in quite plainly. There was a Polar-Bear crouching on the floor, and the head looked at him so directly and vindictively that if he had not been a hero he would have fled. The unexpected is always terrible, and when one goes forth to kill a Giant it is unkind of Providence to complicate one's adventure with a gratuitous and wholly unnecessary Polar-Bear. He was, however, reassured by the sight of a heavy chair standing on the Polar-Bear's stomach, and in the chair there sat the Most-Beautiful-Woman-In-The-World.

An ordinary person would not have understood, at first sight, that she was the Most-Beautiful-Woman-In-The-World, because she looked very stout and much older than is customary with Princesses – but that was because she was under an enchantment and she would become quite young again when the giant was slain and three drops of his blood had been sprinkled on her Brow.

She was leaning forward in her chair staring into the fire, and she was so motionless that he was certain she must be under an enchantment. From the very instant he saw the Princess he loved her, and his heart swelled with pity to think that so beautiful a damsel should be subject to the tyranny of a giant, and these twin passions of pity and love grew to so furious a strength within him that he could no longer contain himself, but wept in a loud and very sudden voice which lifted the damsel out of her enchantment and her chair and hurled her across the room as though she had been propelled by a powerful spring.

He was so overjoyed at seeing her move that he pressed his face against the glass and wept with great strength, and in a few moments the Princess came timidly to the window and looked out. She looked right over his head at first and then she looked down and saw him, and her eyebrows went far up on her forehead and her mouth opened, and so he knew she was delighted to see him. He nodded to give her courage and shouted three times – Open Sesame, Open Sesame, Open Sesame, and then she opened the window and he climbed in. The Princess tried to push him out again, but she was not able, and he bade her put all her jewels in the heel of her boot and fly with him. But she was evidently the victim of a very powerful enchantment, for she struggled violently and said incomprehensible things to him, such as, 'Is it a fire, or were you chased?' and 'Where *is* the cook?' But after a little time she listened to the voice of reason and knew that these were legitimate and heroic embraces from which she could not honourably disentangle herself.

When her first transports of joy were somewhat abated she assured him that excessive haste had often undone great schemes, and that one should look before one leaped, and that one should never be rescued all at once, but gradually, in order that one might become accustomed to the severe air of freedom, and he was overjoyed to find that she was as wise as she was beautiful. He told her that he loved her dearly, and she admitted, after some persuasion, that she was not insensible to the charms of his heart and intellect, but that her love was given to Another. At these tidings his heart withered away within him, and when the Princess admitted that she loved the Giant his amazement became profound and complicated. There was a rushing sound in his ears, the debris of his well-known world was crashing about him and he was staring upon a new planet the name of which was Astonishment. He looked around with a queer feeling of insecurity. At any moment the floor might stand up on one of its corners or the walls might begin to flap and waggle. But none of these things happened. Before him sat the Princess in an attitude of deep dejection and her lily-white hands rested helplessly in her lap. She told him in a voice that trembled that she would have married him if he had asked ten years earlier and said she could not fly with him because, in the first place, she had six children, and, in the second place, it would be against the Law, and, in the third place, his mother might object. She admitted that she was Unworthy of his love and that she should have Waited, and she bore his reproaches with a meekness that finally disarmed him.

He stropped his penknife on his boot and said that there was nothing left but to kill the giant, and that she had better leave the room while he did so because it was not a sight for a weak woman, and he wondered how much hasty-pudding would fall out of the giant if he Stabbed Him Right To The Heart. The Princess begged him not to kill her husband, and assured him that this giant had not got any hasty-pudding in his heart, and stated that he was really the nicest giant who every lived, and that he had *not* killed her seven brothers but the seven brothers of quite another person entirely, which was a reasonable thing to do in the circumstances; and she continued in a strain which proved to him that this unnatural woman really loved the giant.

It was more in pity than in anger that he recognised the impossibility of rescuing this person. He saw at last that she was Unworthy of Being Rescued, and told her so. He said bitterly that he had grave doubts of her being a Princess at all and that if she was married to a giant it was no more than she deserved, and that he had a good mind to rescue the giant from her, and he would do it in a minute only that it was against his principles to rescue giants. And saying so he placed his penknife between his teeth and climbed out through the window.

He stood for a moment outside the window with his right hand extended to the sky and the moonlight blazing on his penknife – a truly formidable figure and one which the Princess never forgot – and then walked slowly away, hiding behind a cold and impassive demeanour a mind that was tortured and a heart that had plumbed most of the depths of human suffering.

Brian Friel (1929-   )
Brian Friel was born in County Tyrone and now lives in County
Donegal. Although he is best known for his plays – among them
Philadelphia, Here I Come!, The Loves of Cass McGuire, Faith Healer and
Translations – he began by writing prose.
Like other stories in this book, 'The Potato Gatherers' was not written
specifically for young people but its description of boys mitching will
bring to mind moments and feelings in the lives of anyone who ever had
to go to school.

The Potato Gatherers
Brian Friel

NOVEMBER FROST HAD STARCHED THE FLAT COUNTRYSIDE into
silent rigidity. The 'rat-tat-tat' of the tractor's exhaust drilled
into the clean, hard air but did not penetrate it; each staccato
sound broke off as if it had been nipped. Hunched over the
driver's wheel sat Kelly, the owner, a rock of a man with a
huge head and broken fingernails, and in the trailer behind
were his four potato gatherers – two young men, permanent
farm hands, and the two boys he had hired for the day. At
six o'clock in the morning, they were the only living things
in that part of County Tyrone.

The boys chatted incessantly. They stood at the front of
the trailer, legs apart, hands in their pockets, their faces
pressed forward into the icy rush of air, their senses edged
for perception. Joe, the elder of the two – he was thirteen
and had worked for Kelly on two previous occasions –might
have been quieter, but his brother's excitement was
infectious. For this was Philly's first job, his first time to take
a day off from school to earn money, his first opportunity to
prove that he was a man at twelve years of age. His energy
was a burden to him. Behind them, on the floor of the
trailer, the two farm hands lay sprawled in half sleep.

Twice the boys had to cheer. The first time was when they
were passing Dicey O'Donnell's house, and Philly, who was
in the same class as Dicey, called across to the thatched,

189

smokeless building, 'Remember me to all the boys, Dicey!'
The second time was when they came to the school itself. It
was then that Kelly turned to them and growled to them to
shut up.

'Do you want the whole country to know you're taking
the day off?' he said. 'Save your breath for your work.'

When Kelly faced back to the road ahead, Philly stuck his
thumbs in his ears, put out his tongue, and wriggled his
fingers at the back of Kelly's head. Then, suddenly
forgetting him, he said, 'Tell me, Joe, what are you going to
buy?'

'Buy?'

'With the money we get today. I know what I'm getting –
a shotgun. Bang! Bang! Bang! Right there, mistah. Jist you
put your two hands up above your head and I reckon you'll
live a little longer.' He menaced Kelly's neck.

'Agh!' said Joe derisively.

'True as God, Joe. I can get it for seven shillings – an old
one that's lying in Tom Tracy's father's barn. Tom told me
he would sell it for seven shillings.'

'Who would sell it?'

'Tom.'

'Steal it, you mean. From his old fella.'

'His old fella has a new one. This one's not wanted.' He
sighted along an imaginary barrel and picked out an
unsuspecting sparrow in the hedge. 'Bang! Never knew
what hit you, did you? What are you going to buy, Joe?'

'I don't know. There won't be much to buy with. Maybe –
naw, I don't know. Depends on what Ma gaves us back.'

'A bicycle, Joe. What about a bike? Quinn would give his
away for a packet of cigarettes. You up on the saddle, Joe,
and me on the crossbar. Out to the millrace every evening.
Me shooting all the rabbits along the way. Bang! Bang!
Bang! What about a bike, Joe?'

'I don't know. I don't know.'

'What did she give you back the last time?'

'I can't remember.'

'Ten shillings? More? What did you buy then? A leather
belt? A set of rabbit snares?'

'I don't think I got anything back. Maybe a shilling. I don't
remember.'

'A shilling! One lousy shilling out of fourteen! Do you know what I'm going to buy? He hunched his shoulders and lowered his head between them. One eye closed in a huge wink. 'Tell no one? Promise?'

'What?'

'A gaff. See?'

'What about the gun?'

'It can wait until next year. But a gaff, Joe. See? Old Philly down there beside the Black Pool. A big salmon. A beaut. Flat on my belly, and – *phwist!* – there he is on the bank, the gaff stuck in his guts.' He clasped his middle and writhed in agony, imitating the fish. Then his act switched suddenly back to cowboys and he drew from both holsters at a cat sneaking home along the hedge. 'Bang! Bang! That sure settled you, boy. Where *is* this potato territory, mistah? Ah want to show you hombres what work is. What's a-keeping this old tractor-buggy?'

'We're jist about there, Mistah Philly, sir said Joe. 'Ah reckon you'll show us, O.K. You'll show us.

The field was a two-acre rectangle bordered by a low hedge. The ridges of potatoes stretched lengthwise in straight, black lines. Kelly unfastened the trailer and hooked up the mechanical digger. The two labourers stood with their hands in their pockets and scowled around them, cigarettes hanging from their lips.

'You two take the far side,' Kelly told them. 'And Joe, you and –' He could not remember the name. 'You and the lad there, you two take this side. You show him what to do, Joe.' He climbed up on the tractor seat. 'And remember,' he called over his shoulder, 'if the school-attendance officer appears, it's up to you to run. I never seen you. I never heard of you.'

The tractor moved forward into the first ridges, throwing up a spray of brown earth behind it as it went.

'Right,' said Joe. 'What we do is this, Philly. When the digger passes, we gather the spuds into these buckets and then carry the buckets to the sacks and fill them. Then back again to fill the buckets. And back to the sacks. O.K., mistah?'

'O.K., mistah. Child's play. What does he want four of us for? I could do the whole field myself—one hand tied

behind my back.'

Joe smiled at him. 'Come on, then. Let's see you.'

'Just you watch,' said Philly. He grabbed a bucket and ran stumbling across the broken ground. His small frame bent over the clay and his thin arms worked madly. Before Joe had begun gathering, Philly's voice called to him. 'Joe! Look! Full already! Not bad, eh?'

'Take your time,' Joe called back.

'And look, Joe! Look!' Philly held his hands out for his brother's inspection. They were coated with earth.

'How's that, Joe? They'll soon be as hard as Kelly's!'

Joe laughed. 'Take it easy, Philly. No rush.'

But Philly was already stooped again over his work, and when Joe was emptying his first bucket into the sack, Philly was emptying his third. He gave Joe the huge wink again and raced off.

Kelly turned at the bottom of the field and came back up. Philly was standing waiting for him.

'What you need is a double digger, Mr Kelly!' he called as the tractor passed. But Kelly's eyes never left the ridges in front of him. A flock of seagulls swooped and dipped behind the tractor, fluttering down to catch worms in the newly turned earth. The boy raced off with his bucket.

'How's it going?' shouted Joe after another twenty minutes. Philly was too busy to answer.

A pale sun appeared about eight-thirty. It was not strong enough to soften the earth, but it loosened sounds – cars along the road, birds in the naked trees, cattle let out for the day. The clay became damp under it but did not thaw. The tractor exulted in its new freedom and its splutterings filled the countryside.

'I've been thinking,' said Philly when he met Joe at a sack. 'Do you know what I'm going to get, Joe? A scout knife with one of those leather scabbards. Four shillings in Byrne's shop. Great for skinning a rabbit.' He held his hands out from his sides now, because they were raw in places. 'Yeah. A scout knife with a leather scabbard.'

'A scout knife,' Joe repeated.

'You always have to carry a scout knife in case your gun won't fire or your powder gets wet. And when you're swimming underwater, you can always carry a knife between

194

your teeth.'

'We'll have near twenty ridges done before noon,' said Joe.

'He should have a double digger. I told him that. Too slow, mistah. Too doggone slow. Tell me, Joe, have you made up your mind yet?'

'What about?'

'What you're going to buy, stupid.'

'Aw, naw. Naw...I don't know yet.'

Philly turned to his work again and was about to begin, when the school bell rang. He dropped his bucket and danced back to his brother. 'Listen! Joe! Listen!' He caught fistfuls of his hair and tugged his head from side to side. 'Listen! Listen! Ha, ha ha! Ho, ho, ho! Come on, you fat, silly, silly scholars and get to your lessons! Come on, come on, come on, come on. No dallying! Speed it up! Get a move on! Hurry! Hurry! Hurry! "And where are the O'Boyle brothers today? Eh? Where are they? Gathering potatoes? What's that I hear? What? What?"'

'Look out, lad!' roared Kelly.

The tractor passed within inches of Philly's legs. He jumped out of its way in time, but a fountain of clay fell on his head and shoulders. Joe ran to his side.

'Are you all right, Philly? Are you O.K.?'

'Tried to get me, that's what he did, the dirty cattle thief. Tried to get me.'

'You O.K., mistah? Reckon you'll live?'

'Sure, mistah. Take more'n that ole coyote to scare me. Come on, mistah. We'll show him what men we really are.' He shook his jacket and hair and hitched up his trousers. 'Would you swap now, Joe?'

'Swap what?'

'Swap places with those poor eejits back there?' He jerked his thumb in the direction of the school.

'No sir,' said Joe. 'Not me.'

'Nor me neither, mistah. Meet you in the saloon.' He swaggered off, holding his hands as if they were delicate things, not part of him.

They broke off for lunch at noon. By then, the sun was high and brave but still of little use. With the engine of the tractor cut off, for a brief time there was a self-conscious

195

silence, which became relaxed and natural when the sparrows, now audible, began to chirp. The seagulls squabbled over the latest turned earth and a cautious puff of wind stirred the branches of the tall trees. Kelly adjusted the digger while he ate. On the far side of the field, the two labourers stretched themselves on sacks and conversed in monosyllables. Joe and Philly sat on upturned buckets. For lunch they each had half a scone of homemade soda bread, cut into thick slices and skimmed with butter. They washed it down with mouthfuls of cold tea from a bottle. After they had eaten, Joe threw the crusts to the gulls, gathered up the newspapers in which the bread had been wrapped, emptied out the remains of the tea, and put the bottle and the papers into his jacket pocket. Then he stood up and stretched himself.

'My back's getting stiff,' he said.

Philly sat with his elbows on his knees and studied the palms of his hands.

'Sore?' asked Joe.

'What?'

'Your hands. Are they hurting you?'

'They're O.K.,' said Philly. 'Tough as leather. But the clay's sore. Gets right into every cut and away up your nails.' He held his arms out. 'They're shaking,' he said. 'Look.'

'That's the way they go,' said Joe. 'But they'll – Listen! Do you hear?'

'Hear what?'

'Lunchtime at school. They must be playing football in the playground.'

The sounds of high, delighted squealing came intermittently when the wind sighed. They listened to it with their heads uplifted, their faces broadening with memory.

'We'll get a hammering tomorrow,' said Joe. 'Six on each hand.'

'It's going to be a scout knife,' Philly said. 'I've decided on that.'

'She mightn't give us anything back. Depends on how much she needs herself.'

'She said she would. She promised. Have you decided yet?'

196

'I'm still thinking,' said Joe.

The tractor roared suddenly, scattering every other sound.

'Come on, mistah,' said the older one. 'Four more hours to go. Saddle up your horse.'

'Coming. Coming,' Philly replied. His voice was sharp with irritation.

The sun was a failure. It held its position in the sky and flooded the countryside with light but could not warm it. Even before it had begun to slip to the west, the damp ground had become glossy again, and before the afternoon was spent, patches of white frost were appearing on higher ground. Now the boys were working automatically, their minds acquiescing in what their bodies did. They no longer straightened up; the world was their feet and the hard clay and the potatoes and their hands and the buckets and the sacks. Their ears told them where the tractor was, at the bottom of the field, turning, approaching. Their muscles had become adjusted to their stooped position, and as long as the boys kept within the established pattern of movement their arms and hands and legs and shoulders seemed to float as if they were free of gravity. But if something new was expected from the limbs – a piece of glass to be thrown in to the hedge, a quick stepping back to avoid the digger – then their bodies shuddered with pain and the tall trees reeled and the hedges rose to the sky.

Dicey O'Donnell gave them a shout from the road on his way home from school. 'Hi! Joe! Philly!'

They did not hear him. He waited until the tractor turned. 'Hi! Hi! Philly! Joe! Youse are for it the morrow. I'm telling youse. He knows where youse are. He says he's going to beat the scruff out of youse the morrow. Youse are in for it, all right. Blue murder! Bloody hell! True as God!'

'Will I put a bullet in him, mistah?' said Joe to Philly.

Philly did not answer. He thought he was going to fall, and his greatest fear was that he might fall in front of the tractor, because now the tractor's exhaust had only one sound, fixed forever in his head, and unless he saw the machine he could not tell whether it was near him or far away. The 'rat-tat-tat' was a finger tapping in his head, drumming at the back of his eyes.

197

'Vamoose, O'Donnell!' called Joe. 'You annoy us. Vamoose.'

O'Donnell said something more about the reception they could expect the next day, but he got tired of calling to two stooped backs and he went off home.

The last pair of ridges was turned when the sky had veiled itself for dusk. The two brothers and the two labourers worked on until they met in the middle. Now the field was all brown, all flat, except for the filled sacks that patterned it. Kelly was satisfied; his lips formed an O and he blew through them as if he were trying to whistle. He detached the digger and hooked up the trailer. 'All aboard!' he shouted, in an effort at levity.

On the way home, the labourers seemed to be fully awake, for the first time since morning. They stood in the trailer where the boys had stood at dawn, behind Kelly's head and facing the road before them. They chatted and guffawed and made plans for a dance that night. When they met people they knew along the way, they saluted extravagantly. At the crossroads, they began to wrestle, and Kelly had to tell them to watch out or they would fall over the side. But he did not sound angry.

Joe sat on the floor, his legs straight out before him, his back resting against the side of the trailer. Philly lay flat out, his head cushioned on his brother's lap. Above him, the sky spread out, grey, motionless, enigmatic. The warmth from Joe's body made him drowsy. He wished the journey home to go on forever, the sound of the tractor engine to anaesthetize his mind forever. He knew that if the movement and the sound were to cease, the pain of his body would be unbearable.

'We're nearly there,' said Joe quietly. 'Are you asleep?' Philly did not answer. 'Mistah! Are you asleep, mistah?'

'No.'

Darkness came quickly, and when the last trace of light disappeared the countryside became taut with frost. The headlamps of the tractor glowed yellow in the cold air.

'Philly! Are you awake, mistah?'

'What?'

'I've been thinking,' said Joe slowly. 'And do you know what I think? I think I've made up my mind now.'

198

One of the labourers burst into song.

' "If I were a blackbird, I'd whistle and sing, and I'd follow the ship that my true love sails in." '

His mate joined him at the second line and their voices exploded in the stiff night.

'Do you know what I'm going to buy?' Joe said, speaking more loudly. 'If she gives us something back, that is. Mistah! Mistah Philly! Are you listening? I'm going to buy a pair of red silk socks.'

He waited for approval from Philly. When none came, he shook his brother's head. 'Do you hear, mistah? Red silk socks – the kind Jojo Teague wears. What about that, eh? What do you think?'

Philly stirred and half raised his head from his brother's lap. 'I think you're daft,' he said in an exhausted, sullen voice. 'Ma won't give us back enough to buy anything much. No more than a shilling. You knew it all the time.' He lay down again and in a moment he was fast asleep.

Joe held his brother's head against the motion of the trailer and repeated the words 'red silk socks' to himself again and again, nodding each time at the wisdom of his decision.

Acknowledgements

Permission to use copyright material is gratefully acknowledged by the editors and The O'Brien Press to the following: Victor Gollancz Ltd., for 'The China Doll' from *The Far Side of the Lough* by Polly Devlin © 1983; Macmillan, London and Basingstoke, for 'Eonín' from *Turf Fire Tales* by Mary Patton; David Higham Associates Ltd., for an excerpt from *Never No More* by Maura Laverty; Constable Publishers, for 'A Likely Story' from *Collected Stories Volume II* by Mary Lavin; A. P. Watt Ltd., for 'The Breadth of a Whisker' by Janet McNeill; Eileen O'Faoláin for 'Cliona, Queen of Muskerry' from *The Little Black Hen*; The estate of Seumas MacManus for 'The Widow's Daughter' from *Hibernian Nights*; The Society of Authors, on behalf of Mrs. Iris Wise, for 'The Unworthy Princess' from *Here Are Ladies* by James Stephens; Chatto and Windus Ltd., for 'A Stocking Full of Gold' from *They Lived in Co. Down* by Kathleen Fitzpatrick; A. P. Watt Ltd., and the author, for 'The Trout' by Seán O'Faoláin; A. D. Peters and Co. Ltd., for 'Weep for Our Pride' from *Collected Stories* by James Plunkett; The estate of Hilton Edwards for 'St. Brigid's Eve' by Micheál mac Liammóir; Eilís Dillon, for her story 'Bad Blood'; The estate of John O'Connor, for his story 'Neilly and the Fir Tree'; A. D. Peters and Co. Ltd., for 'First Confession' from *Stories of Frank O'Connor* published by Hamish Hamilton; copyright to the introduction by Eilís Dillon and 'The Potato Gatherers' by Brian Friel and the translations of *Jimín Mháire Thaidhg* and 'M'Asal Beag Dubh' is held by The O'Brien Press.

Every effort has been made to contact copyright holders; we would be happy to amend any oversight.

OTHER BOOKS FROM THE O'BRIEN PRESS

THE HUNTER'S MOON
Orla Melling

Adventure, mystery, and the sorcery and magic of the Other World combine when Findabhair disappears and her cousin Gwen sets out to find her.

£3.99 pb

THE DRUID'S TUNE
Orla Melling

Caught up in the enchantments of a modern-day druid, Rosemary and Jimmy are hurled into the ancient past. They have the adventure of their lives in the unusual company of Cuchulainn and Queen Maeve.

£4.50 pb

CELTIC MAGIC TALES
Liam MacUistin

Four magical legends from Ireland's Celtic past: the Tuatha de Danann and their king's love-quest; a fantastic and humorous tale of Cuchulainn; the story of Deirdre and the Sons of Usnach; the heroic tale of the Sons of Tuireann.

£3.99 pb

THE TÁIN
Liam MacUistin

The great classic Celtic tale, full of the excitement of the battle, and ending with the terrible fight to the death between best friends Cuchulainn and Ferdia.

£5.95 hb /£3.95pb

AMELIA
Siobhán Parkinson

The year is 1914 and there are rumours of war in the air. But all that matters to Amelia is what she will wear to her thirteenth birthday party. But when disaster strikes her family, Amelia must hold them together.

£3.99 pb

STAR DANCER
Morgan Llywelyn

When Ger breaks into the RDS horse show, he sees a new world, and he desperately wants to be part of it. Suzanne, riding her horse Star Dancer, has a target too: she wants to train for the Olympics. Their dreams overlap, with interesting results.

£3.99 pb

BRIAN BORU
Morgan Llywelyn

The most famous of Ireland's heroes – this is his life story from childhood to the Battle of Clontarf.

£3.95 pb

STRONGBOW
Morgan Llywelyn

The dramatic story of the arrival in Ireland of the Normans, and of Strongbow's life with his new wife, the young Irish princess Aoife. Vivid and exciting history with a strong story.

£3.99 pb

UNDER THE HAWTHORN TREE
Marita Conlon-McKenna

The heartfelt, dramatic account of the children of the Great Irish Famine – Eily, Michael and Peggy – who make a long journey on their own to find the great-aunts they have heard about in their mother's stories.

£3.95 pb

WILDFLOWER GIRL
Marita Conlon-McKenna

Peggy, now thirteen, sets out for America to find a new life. She goes into service in a large Boston house, and must find her own feet in the difficult world of the emigrant.

£4.50 pb

THE BLUE HORSE
Marita Conlon-McKenna

When Katie's family's home burns down they are left destitute. Now she must find a way to hold the family together and must try to fit into a completely new life. But will she be accepted?

£3.99 pb

HORSE THIEF
Hugh Galt

Rory's old horse is stolen, and to prevent it happening again he runs away with her in the night. But they soon come across another horse hidden in the depths of the country. Then begins the wildest chase, in an attempt to save both horses.

£3.99 pb

BIKE HUNT
Hugh Galt

Niall Quinn's new bike is stolen and he is determined to find it. Helped by the skill of Katie, and by his friend Paudge, Niall becomes entangled in a dangerous situation in the Wicklow Mountains.

£3.95 pb

THE CASTLE IN THE ATTIC
Elizabeth Winthrop

There is a strange legend attached to the model castle given to William by Mrs Phillips. He is drawn into the story when the silver knight who guards the castle comes to life.

£3.99 pb

THE LOST ISLAND
Eilís Dillon

Is the lost island real or fantasy? And who is brave enough to try to find it and gain the treasure? Michael and Joe set off in their boat to reveal the secret of the island.

£3.95 pb

THE CRUISE OF THE SANTA MARIA
Eilís Dillon

John sets sail in a splendid Galway hooker, ending up on a deserted island, empty except for one unusual inhabitant. Here begins a strange adventure, full of excting, tense moments.

£4.50 pb

OTHER WORLD SERIES

OCTOBER MOON
Michael Scott

Rachel Stone and her family are scared by weird happenings at their stables in Kildare. But is it the locals trying to get rid of them or something more sinister?

£3.99 pb

GEMINI GAME
Michael Scott

BJ and Liz O'Connor are gamemakers, but when their virtual reality computer game Night's Castle develops a bug, they risk their lives to try to solve the problem. An exciting futuristic novel.

£3.99 pb

HOUSE OF THE DEAD
Michael Scott

Something goes very wrong when Claire and Patrick go to Newgrange on their school tour. Can they find a way to keep the evil powers they have released from destroying the whole of Ireland?

£3.99 pb

MOONLIGHT
Michael Carroll

Moonlight is not just an ordinary horse. His owner dreams he will be the fastest racehorse ever. But Cathy intervenes, and the result is a tense, nail-biting chase for survival.

£3.99 pb

OTHER BOOKS FOR YOUNGER CHILDREN

Dingwell Street School Stories
RUBBERNECK'S REVENGE
Martin Waddell

Illustrated by Arthur Robins

Ernie Flack and his friends find themselves in Heap Big Trouble when the Deputy Head goes on the warpath in this action-packed Dingwell Street School story.

£3.50 pb

THE FISHFACE FEUD
Martin Waddell

Illustrated by Arthur Robins

The honour of class P6 is at stake when Ernie Flack and friends take on Fishface Duggan and his gang from P7 in this lively story.

£3.50 pb

THE SCHOOL THAT WENT TO SEA
Martin Waddell

Illustrated in full colour by Leo Hartas

Imagine if it rained so hard your school floated away, like a ship, out to sea. That is what happens in this story – and everyone is very pleased that they have a clever teacher like Ms Smith on board to guide them.

£3.99 pb

LITTLE STAR
Marita Conlon-McKenna

Illustrated in full colour by Christopher Coady

A first picture book from Ireland's favourite author. A story for little ones – a tale of intimacy, feeling and charm.

6.99 hb

Off We Go . . . 1
THE DUBLIN ADVENTURE
Siobhán Parkinson

Illustrated by Cathy Henderson

Dara and his big sister Sinéad are in Dublin for the first time. City life is new to them, with all its strange ways. A witty and informative account of a first visit to Dublin.

£3.99 pb

Off We Go . . . 2
THE COUNTRY ADVENTURE
Siobhán Parkinson

Illustrated by Cathy Henderson

Michelle lives in Dublin and knows a thing or two. She knows that country people are a bit peculiar. But when she visits Sinéad and Dara, her country cousins, she discovers she has a lot to learn.
A funny and revealing look at life on a farm through the eyes of a young city-slicker.

£3.99 pb

THE LEPRECHAUN WHO WISHED HE WASN'T
Siobhán Parkinson

Laurence is a leprechaun who has been small for 1100 years and is sick of it! He wants to be TALL. He wants to be cool. Then he meets Phoebe, a large girl who wants to be small.
A tall tale indeed.

£3.99 pb

THAT PEST JONATHAN
William Cole

Illustrated by Tomi Ungerer

The thing that Jonathan liked best was being a pest! Or so it seemed to his parents, so they took him to see Doctor Carrother. But his answer to their little problem is unexpected.

£2.99 pb

WHIZZ QUIZ
Seán O'Leary

Illustrated by Ann O'Leary

Chockful of quizzes and fantastic puzzles on every topic under the sun. Great fun – and educational too!

£2.99 pb

THE O'BRIEN PRESS, 20 VICTORIA ROAD, DUBLIN 6, IRELAND

Add to total, 15% for postage, 25% for airmail

I enclose cheque/postal order for £......
Please charge my credit card ☐ ACCESS ☐ MASTERCARD ☐ VISA

Card:

Expiry:

Name...... *St Brigids School*
Address...... *Killester.*

All these books are available from your local bookseller. In case of difficulty order directly from The O'Brien Press